MW00962532

THE FLESH SO CLOSE

BOOKS BY KENNETH J. HARVEY:

Directions for an Opened Body (1990)
Brud (1992)
The Hole That Must Be Filled (1994)
Stalkers (1994)
Kill the Poets (1995)
Nine-Tenths Unseen (1996)
The Great Misogynist (1996)
Everyone Hates a Beauty Queen (1998)
The Woman in the Closet (1998)
The Flesh So Close (1998)

the flesh so close

Stories

KENNETH J. HARVEY

THE MERCURY PRESS

Copyright © 1998 by Island Horse Productions Limited

ALL RIGHTS RESERVED. No part of this book may be reproduced by any means without the prior written permission of the publisher, with the exception of brief passages in reviews. Any request for photocopying or other reprographic copying of any part of this book must be directed in writing to the Canadian Reprography Collective (CANCOPY).

The publisher gratefully acknowledges the financial assistance of the Canada Council for the Arts and the Ontario Arts Council. The publisher further acknowledges the support of the Department of Canadian Heritage through the BPIDP.

Cover design by Gordon Robertson
Edited by Beverley Daurio
Composition and page design by TASK

Printed and bound in Canada by Metropole Litho
Printed on acid-free paper
First Edition
1 2 3 4 5   02 01 00 99 98

Canadian Cataloguing in Publication Data

Harvey, Kenneth J. (Kenneth Joseph), 1962-
The flesh so close

ISBN 1-55128-062-0
I. Title.
PS8565.A678F53 1998   C813'.54   C98-932205-X
PR9199.3.H37F53 1998

Represented in Canada by the Literary Press Group
Distributed in Canada by General Distribution Services

THE MERCURY PRESS Toronto, Canada M6P 2A7

for old friends
taken too soon:

Austin "Bud" Greene
and
Mark King

and for:

Bill and Dede Gaston
(never get out of the van)

contents

Lightning Dust

In my dream, I find myself visiting a chiropractor. The cramped waiting room is filled with pigeons in tiny neck braces. I turn to my pregnant wife and say, "That's what they get for walking the way they do. They should know better."

My wife's breasts are growing deliciously larger by the moment, occupying more space, billowing across the waiting area. "What's there to do about this Imperialist Boob Syndrome of yours? Your breasts keep getting bigger and bigger. You're the proverbial Mother Land."

I am smiling. I cannot make the smile go away. The corners of my mouth hurt and my jaw aches. When I awake, I am chuckling. Rolling over in bed, I explore the crumpled sheets, the desolate plain beside me. I have no wife. I have no spinal problem in need of treatment. The dream is not funny. It is pathetic.

Sitting up, I swing my legs over the side of the bed and stare across the bedroom to where my dog is lying by the veranda door that leads out and down into the back yard.

"Hey, Mope," I glumly call, making a brief, non-committal sound with my lips.

His ears twitch, the left one, then the right, before one of his wrinkled eyelids slowly opens.

"Let's find us a wife today, hey, boy?"

Mope's second eye opens and then— as if the strain is absolutely too much for him— both of his lids collapse.

I tell myself, "Matthew should be awake by now." Quieting my thoughts and listening beyond my body, I hear my son singing from his room off the upstairs hallway.

"Daddy," his bright quick voice calls out, "I've got something to show you."

"Okay," I tell him, rubbing my bare toes back and forth along the forest-green carpet, making it darker or lighter by brushing in different directions. I write the letter "M" with my big toe, and wonder about the day before me. Will my thoughts near occasion in the coming hours?

I hear Matthew jump down from his bed. The soft thump and then the hard and short strides of his small legs as they bring him closer to my room. When I look toward the doorway, I see him standing there in his zip-up pajamas, pausing to examine a glossy, colourful piece of paper he holds in his hands. He is smiling down at the paper when he says, "Good morning."

Mope feigns attentiveness, lifting his head slightly to give Matthew a quiet look. Content that nothing too extravagant is passing without his notice, he lets his head thud back down onto the carpet.

"Look," says Matthew, hurrying toward the bed and climbing up. The glossy sheet of paper rattles in his hand. Standing on the mattress, he steps close to my side, and points at a picture of a toy pirate ship with movable pirate figures. "See that?"

"Yes, I see it." Studying the promotional flyer, I feel a heavy weight drop onto the foot of the bed. The weight settles instantly and does not move again. When I look out from behind the images of pirate ships, I see that Mope is lying on the bed covers, his brow lifting, his eyes only slightly open, watching me for an instant before blowing air out the corners of his flabby mouth.

"That's what I want for my birthday," Matthew insists, pointing, then leaning his small arm around my shoulders and twirling my hair.

"What birthday?"

Matthew laughs and falls back onto the bed, bouncing as he lands on his bum with his legs up in the air. His blonde hair catches the morning light, and his white skin holds a slight shade of pink high in his cheeks. "My birthday," he tells me, rolling his sharp blue eyes up into his head. Quickly he scrambles to stand and playfully slaps my arm. "My birthday. Tomorrow. My birthday. You know? It's my birthday, the day I was born." He nods and nods at me, then pauses dramatically, sighs deeply and laughs, throwing his hands up to cover his face before pouncing on my back. Growling, he wrestles me down onto the bed.

"Aw, cute little Mope with the face." Matthew kneels close to the dog, rubbing and kissing Mope's leathery loose-skinned head. The dog lies on the living-room carpet in a wide bar of sunlight, soaking up the cosy heat.

Secretively, I lift the channel changer from the top of the television and slip the narrow length of it into my back pocket. I pull this off undetected. Then I stroll across the living room toward the yellow and green plaid couch.

"Watch this," I say, my voice turning deep and mystical. "The Great Zamzoodles will now perform." Matthew looks at me and I carefully point my sorcerer's finger at the blank screen.

"Pow," I shout, jabbing my finger in the air while pressing the remote control's "on" button behind my back.

Matthew's face lights up as the sound and picture fade in. He stares at the screen, enthralled by the gradual appearance of an image. Once he sees what program is on, he hugs the dog enthusiastically, cheering, "My Dad's magic!"

"No sweat," I say. "You watch a bit of television, okay? I've got to make a call." I do not wait for an answer. He is a good boy; he does not question what I ask of him.

Out in the kitchen, I run my finger down the yellow pages, reading each line, then studying the corresponding advertisements. The women working for these companies will do absolutely anything for a fee (it says so in the fine print in a roundabout way) so I see no reason why one of them would not be willing to play mommy for half a day.

When I dial the number, a sultry voice purrs from the other end, "Peaches Escort Service."

"Hello," I say, trying to sound as vibrant and normal as possible.

"What can we do for you?"

"It says here you accept credit cards; that's an accurate statement, is it? I can believe it to be the truth?"

The satiny voice laughs, a careful good-natured laugh. "Yes, sir. We accept all major credit cards."

"Good. What I'm looking for is an escort to be my wife for an afternoon. A birthday party."

"Certainly. That won't be a problem at all. We have many women who specialize in such assignments."

I am surprised. "Really!? That's great." I guess I am not the only one with such involved needs.

"Is it a private party? One on one, or...?"

"No, a family party."

"Family, ahhh. I see what you're after."

"Just an escort, nothing other than that. For my boy. For his birthday. He's..." I stop myself from giving his age, realizing the confusion that is mounting. To say his age would imply certain unsavoury things that I do not intend.

"We can arrange that. Certainly. Could you please state your preferences with regards to the type of lady you wish to escort you to this party?"

"One who looks the part."

"Oh, they can all look the part, sir. What I meant was, do you prefer a certain hair colour, or height, weight, skin shade?" She mechanically announces several other attributes, as if reading from a list. She makes everything sound so orderly and habitual.

"It's strictly a Platonic thing," I tell her, outlining my preferences, or rather the intricate characteristics that I believe Matthew would favour in a mommy. After all, it is his birthday.

Running through my choice of select features, with the sultry voice listening at the other end, I find that I am assembling what was once already mine. I thought I had purged myself of her image, but she is there in the descriptive words that spill spontaneously from my mouth: none other than the woman I lost years ago. I remember, and the telephone receiver feels hard against my lips. My voice falters. But my voice will not leave me alone. It speaks inside my head. It pronounces her name. Katherine.

"Good night," I whisper into the dimness of Matthew's bedroom. His night light is on, and I understand how he finds it so reassuring.

"Night, Daddy," he says, his arms out over the cartoon-character quilt. "I love you."

"I love you, too, pal."

"See you in the morning."

"Don't take any wooden dreams."

Matthew buries his head in his pillow and giggles.

"Hey, I forgot. I've got something here in my pocket for you."

My son lifts his head and stares at me in utter silence. "What is it?"

"Can't say." I see him sitting up in bed, arranging himself in a comfortable position. I hesitate for a moment, pressing my lips together and shaking my head doubtfully. "I don't know if you're ready for this sort of thing."

"For what?"

Leaning against the wall, I reach back with my right arm, feel for the light switch, find it, but do not flick it on. I simply hold it between my thumb and index finger, ready. My eyes begin to adjust to the dimness and I can see Matthew's expectant position more clearly.

"What?" he says, stirred by childish impatience. He slaps at the bed covers with his hands. "Is it a squirt in the face with the water squirter? Is that what it is? Go ahead, then. Go on."

He folds his arms and tilts back his head, then he stares at my hand and how it digs in my pocket.

"It's down here pretty deep," I tell him.

"What is it?" He bounces slightly on his bum.

"Ahhhh! Ah-hah! Ah-heh! Ah-hah! Here it is." I pull out my hand and hold my tightly closed fist straight out in front of me. "Lightning dust," I say, pausing for effect, letting the words linger in the air to come apart and sparkle in memory.

"Show me," Matthew laughs.

"Are you ready?"

"Yes."

"Are you sure."

"Yes, yes."

I open my hand, flicking my fingers, throwing the imaginary dust at him and making a magical wind-whooshing sound with my mouth. At the same instant, and with one swift movement, I jerk the light switch up and down using my other hand, the yellow flash bursting against our eyes, then dwindling, seeping back, deeper into us as our bodies once again face dimness.

"Wow!" Matthew croons. "Lightning dust."

"You like that?"

"Yes. Do it again please, Daddy."

"I don't know. It's really rare stuff."

"Please?"

"Mmmmmm, I don't know."

"Please!?"

"Okay," I give in to the pressure. "But just once more. Wouldn't want to spoil you with all this magic."

I reach in and pull out another secret handful, toss it into the air and pulse the light. Then I stand there in the vague glow of his night light, watching my son's wondrous smile. He does not say a word. He is utterly amazed. And so am I; enthralled by my ability to set such pure and breathless marvel in the vivid thoughts that race through Matthew's mind.

Mope does not bother barking when the doorbell sounds. He just slides his head along the carpet, pointing his wet rubbery nostrils toward the source of the noise.

I walk for the front door and open it. The woman stands outside on the concrete landing. She smiles a kind smile and her eyes turn extremely narrow with sincerity.

"Hi," I say, somewhat startled by the authenticity of her appearance. I remain silent for several moments, my arms and legs gone numb. I cannot pull my eyes away from her remarkable face. It is exactly what I had in mind. Exactly.

The woman makes the first move and I must snap out of my trance, excuse myself and step aside, holding the door for her as she enters. "Come in. It's good to see you again." I give her a kiss on the cheek and glance down the hallway to see Matthew peeking out from the kitchen. His hair is combed perfectly to the side, on the same slant that my bang is combed (he always asks to have it done this way) and he is wearing a little blue blazer, a blue bow-tie, white shirt, red suspenders, blue short pants and black buckle-up shoes with white socks. All brand new, bought yesterday for the special occasion.

"Hello, Norman. It's good to see you, too. It's been a while." The woman takes her coat off and smooths the fabric of her paisley dress along her waist. The material is hunter green with highlights of deep red and hints of muted gold. Underneath the dress she wears a plain white blouse with only one button unfastened at the collar.

"Yes." I take her coat and hang it on the wall rack, quite pleased by her casualness, the poise of each gesture.

"You haven't seen Matthew since he was a baby," I say, perhaps in a tone of slight accusation. The remark could easily have been interpreted as such, rather than taken as intended: as a piece of simple information. Small talk. Chit chat. "Have you, Katherine?" I wink at her, but she does not even react to the signal. She requires no prodding.

"No, that's right. Where is he? Where's my little angel?"

I think, Wow! Has she got it down!

This woman I call Katherine turns away from me to search the hallway. She smiles quietly when she sees Matthew scamper off, retreating into the kitchen.

"He's back there," I tell her. "Everything's already laid out for the party."

Matthew is sitting at the table when Katherine and I step in.

"Matthew, this is Katherine."

"Hi," he says, wiping his mouth with the clown-faced paper napkin beside his plate. A few crumbs from his peanut butter and jam sandwich have fallen onto the placemat and Katherine moves over there to brush them into her palm, all the while watching Matthew. Then she leans closer and kisses him on the cheek.

"Hi, honey," she says, sweeping the crumbs onto his plate. "How're you doing on your birthday?" She takes an important look at the cake on the table, then glances back at Matthew's face. "Five years old today. You're a big boy."

Matthew nods. "Yes." He is proud of himself. Five years old means a great deal to him. "See the balloons." He points at the walls where red, green and orange balloons cling in place, held there by static electricity from being rubbed against my hair.

Katherine picks up a party hat and sets it on her head, carefully pulling the thin elastic down under her chin. "How does that look?" Then she raises a swirled party favour and blows it at Matthew. It quickly unfurls like a frog's tongue and the yellow feathers at the tip tickle Matthew's lips. Frantically he wipes at his face and laughs.

"You're ready for all kinds of surprises. Today, I mean. Your birthday." The woman lays down the party favour and reaches into the deep front pocket of her dress. Lifting out a little box wrapped in purple paper with a pale blue bow on top, she holds it out to the birthday boy and smiles.

"It's for you, sweetie," she says.

Matthew looks back at me.

"Go ahead," I tell him. "It's okay. You can open mine later."

Without further hesitation, he tears the wrapper off the box and opens it up. Inside, there is a silver locket on a silver chain resting against a lining of deep blue velvet.

"It opens," she says, using her sleek fingernails to pry it apart. "See." She holds the tiny photograph toward him so he can have a closer look.

"It's Dad, and you!" Matthew says. "Wow!" He takes the locket from Katherine's hand and turns it so I can view the photograph. It would be a lie to say I am not struck by the potency of similar memories.

Katherine regards me. She sees what I am thinking, but she only sees it for a moment before Matthew pulls her gaze away. Grabbing hold of her hand, he drags her from the kitchen. "Come and see my room," he insists. Hurrying ahead down the hallway, he waves his arm above his head, his smile more joyful than any expression yet to grace his boyishly handsome face.

Katherine laughs in a pleasing manner and follows him without even giving me a glance. I leave them alone, turn away and sit at the kitchen table. In his haste, Matthew has left the locket on the table, and I stare down at what the photograph has captured. The woman looks the part, so very close to the genuine article. So very very close that it makes me wonder, compels me to think of a past I do not wish to recall.

She even took the time to bring along the photograph. How clever! The man in the image could easily be a younger me. I am convinced. It could be me, and the woman is definitely her. There is no mistake. So giving and gentle. Her approach is enticing, and I try to leave it at that, not wanting to speculate about her background. I must veer away from thoughts that threaten to mar the consummate innocence of the situation. All of this is for Matthew, not for me. The boy's birthday is the highlight of this day.

I stare at the cake and count the candles. They are set apart, a certain distance between them. One. Two. Three. Four. Five years.

Matthew is playing "Three Blind Mice" on his toy piano for Katherine. A few moments later I hear him slowly reading the alphabet from the chart on his wall, then spelling his name for her, then reciting the digits of his phone number that I taught him, informing her of his street address, how much he weighs, then yanking out the drawers of his dresser and showing Katherine all his clothes and telling the story behind each article.

I stand close to the stairway and listen to the rush of information that Matthew must relay to Katherine. I realize that he has learned all of this from me. His anxiousness and delight in expressing himself to this woman makes me aware that he is merely translating my desire to pass the very same information on to her. He is the heart of my need to be proud of what I do and have done in our home.

In a short while, they both leave the bedroom and move down the upstairs hallway toward the stairway. Matthew is still talking, without pause.

I quietly dash back into the kitchen, take a seat, cross my legs, and close the locket as if to deny any interest in it. I hear Matthew laughing at something that Katherine has said. He races down the stairs ahead of her, but then pauses and calls out, waiting for her to catch up.

I watch them come in through the kitchen archway. They are smiling and holding hands. They are both looking at me as they enter. Matthew rushes over to the table and takes the locket, slips the chain around his neck, and pops it open. The chain is too long for him, so he holds up the locket, looks at it, then turns it toward me. I stare at the photograph, not wanting to recognize it, but needing to, for his sake.

"That was quite a day, a picnic," I tell him. Then I say something that I have no means of fully understanding, "The day you were conceived."

"He certainly is a wonderful boy," says Katherine, her eyes smiling in the corners, her lips rising obligingly. Sweeping her long brown hair back over her shoulders, she adds, "You must be very proud."

"This is great, Dad," Matthew beams, rapidly taking hold of Katherine's hand again and looking at how he is holding it. He is proud of himself, as if he has accomplished something of great importance by having this woman here among us.

"Pictures," I say to Matthew.

He nods with a huge smile.

I stand, then lift the camera from the table, raise it up to my eye, find them there, centre them, step back away from how they wait there so calmly, centre them again, evenly, so that no one could ever claim that the composition is off-balance.

Then I press the button. The flash goes off and they blink in unison, standing perfectly still, as if some miraculous clarity has been fired through them, erasing history for a brief moment.

"Now you and Katherine," pipes Matthew, running over and pulling the camera from my hands.

I try to hold onto the hard black casing, but Matthew is suddenly stronger than me and has yanked the camera away. I stare down at him, see that he is smiling in an apologetic way. I muss up his hair, then move toward the counter. Katherine welcomes me gladly, shifting closer and slipping her arm around my waist. I slip mine over her slim shoulders and we both smile for him.

"Make sure you can see the two of us," I instruct Matthew.

He moves the camera slightly to the left, then slightly to the right.

"I see you," he says. "Both of you are there."

"Tell us when," I say, trying to hold my smile. It is an effort, and I must work to extend the moment. "Make sure so that we're ready."

Katherine gently rubs the side of my waist with her fingertips and leans her head against my shoulder.

"When," calls Matthew, the flash going off.

"Another one," he says right away.

I imagine him peeking out from behind the camera. In the wake of the flash's brilliance, I cannot see him at all. He is washed-out and lost there somewhere in my field of vision.

"Okay, Daddy? Can I?"

When I tell him okay, he will put himself behind the viewfinder again and find us. "When," he will say, pressing the button, the flash pulsing, burning into our eyes so that I have an urge to shield myself. "When," he will say. "When, when..."

I have another dream that no one would ever care to embrace. It happens the night after Katherine has left, she and my son having kissed each other goodbye and pledged to get together in the very near future; a pledge that I must promise to guide to fruition.

The dream is totally unbelievable, and I wonder what would be the sense of explaining it. It has to do with pigeons, my dream hinting at how these birds rarely fly away, how they are not afraid of being extremely near to you, how they will never lift off from the place that they have settled in unless they sense the prospect of terrible danger, a closeness that threatens their very lives.

I know that my dreams try to tell me something. But interpretation is a virtual impossibility, for dreams are there one minute and gone the next. They change without reason or the slightest warning, leaving you confounded and dumb-struck in your soul.

In this new dream I am no longer at the chiropractor hoping to have my spine straightened. I am at Peaches Escort Service and all of the women appear alike. A hundred Katherines stand before me and they are all pregnant, with large breasts and motherly faces that aim to please the future generations they nurture in their wombs.

Slowly becoming conscious of my own body, I realize that I am holding a tiny hand. Peering down, I see that Matthew is smiling up at me, saying, "Wow! This is great, Dad." Then he gazes ahead again, marvelling at all the mommies in front of him, positioned up the wooden stairway and down the red and pink hall.

As if on cue, the lights begin to dim and, just when I think it will soon be absolutely dark, lightning flashes through the room. It is then that I realize my other hand is resting on the switch. I am looking at my fingers. They bend and straighten loosely in a helpless way that implies I have absolutely no control over the light thrown upon this scene.

When I turn to face the front again, each of the women is holding up a camera and aiming to capture us, as if we are the evasive ones whom they must contend to preserve. Multiple images of my son and I are reflected back at us from their many lenses. We are motionless and unconnected. But then, something clicks, countless shutters opening at once, and we are defined and taken whole.

Lowering their cameras, the women move toward us, raising the colour photographs that have appeared in their hands, showing them and nodding in a charitable way, as if offering coins to the poor. But they do not realize the images are depthless, transitory, a superficial catharsis. I am without expression in the glossy eight-by-ten portraits, but Matthew is smiling nicely in an earnest and open-hearted way. My son is quite pleased with where he has found himself, in this infinitely loving spell of magic, where people would still trade anything to avoid the heartbreakingly human withdrawal of touch.

St. John's, 1992

Merciful Hope

for Josiah Boyde Harvey

The bridge was made from wood slats loosely set side by side so that they rattled beneath the wheels of the pick-up trucks that drove across. Dust would rise in the wake of the vehicles, lifting in slow lingering clouds from the backwoods road just outside Cutland Junction. But rain had come the previous night and the ground was damp and packed tight; a sweet musty odour lingered in the air. Beneath the bridge, water ran high along the river's banks, the surface murky from churned-up sediment.

Muss appeared from the woods, ducking out onto the road, his young face looking like a lumpy sack of potatoes, his black hair curly and coarse and set mostly on the top of his head. The twiggy bushes rustled and Muss stopped, turning to watch, until the old half-breed beagle hobbled clear, its sad eyes staring ahead from where it stood, low to the ground, no more than five feet behind the skinny legs of its master, standing in wait.

Satisfied with sighting the dog, Muss strolled close to the bridge, glancing back to view the wasted body pushing on to follow obediently.

The mongrel came to him as he bent to tie the rope around its throat, the dog's warm eyes shining soft in the dusk, its ribs aching out from its mottled fur, its ears softly laid back as the knot was roughly tied. Muss glanced around his feet, then up the gravel road that led on in to the Junction. Spotting something, he wandered back. But the dog did not follow. It sat and watched, yawned elaborately, then shook its head, its leathery ears flapping.

Muss' voice came first, returning from the distance: "Keep dem eyes ahf me."

The dog whined, a tiny squeal trapped in its throat.

"N'ver know why." He bent and coiled the other end of the coarse rope around a slab-shaped boulder that had been cracked in two. "T'ings like ya in ever'n's kitchen, ly'n 'round, do'n nut'n. Eat'n 'n' do'n nut'n. I tol' ya all dis 'fore. Dun't lees'n."

He tied a knot and then another, pulling with his hands, tugging the splintery rope to make certain it was set steady around the rock. "Dere." Standing, he blew the fibres from his hands, then shoved them into his pockets. He stared up the road, a tired glimmer in his eyes, as if hoping someone might drive along and offer casual greeting or a worthwhile piece of advice, but the road was deserted, lined with tall black evergreens and blonde spotted birch and the light was wasting away, growing toward the suffocating darkness that closed in so softly.

Muss listened to the river. He heard the sound of it rising up to mingle and find itself at home with this kind of light so that it sounded clearer, forceful. He pulled a package of Export "A" from the pocket of his blue work shirt and stuck his thumb into the bottom of the pack, pushing up. Digging down with two fingers, he lifted out a bent, black-tipped butt, and flipped the lid of his father's old Zippo, the smell of it never failing to please him.

"Sit'n' dere like dat," he said, puffing with the flame rising so close to his lips he had to work fast, the heat full against him. He leaned back and snapped the lighter shut, a lingering orange wash in his eyes. He shoved the package into his front pocket. "May'b' dis'll help ya run." Squatting down, he cuddled the dog and the boulder in both his arms and stood, holding the weight only long enough to receive its impression before tossing it forward.

He had expected the sound of a large splash and a smaller muddled plunk, but there was only one sound of water rushing up. Not a sound from the dog. Not a yelp or a moan, only the dim sight of it dropping through the air with its eyes opened and its legs not even kicking, its paws bent and tucked in close to its white and brown chest.

The sound of the river was turning louder as darkness steadily sealed itself. Muss stood on the bridge with no railings, then inched close to the edge to watch the deep water. It was only water, he told himself. Nothing moving down there. There were rumours that at night, as the river blackened, the bottom slowly fell out and what was thrown in there would find its way down into the blind rush that led away, carrying things to a place of calm and contentment.

Flicking his cigarette into the flow, he imagined the whispering sizzle it would make when it hit. But even the sound of this was denied him. He glanced around and decided that the night was turning its back on all his intentions. It would never forgive him, nor welcome the convictions he had settled on. He heard his stomach grumble, but did not feel the movement in his gut. It was merely a murmur coming from a remote place in the dark that he had learned to hold away from himself. Leaning as he was, staring down into the wet rushing shadows, he backed away for fear he would fall into the water. It drew him sometimes, knowing what it was there for, what it was meant to take away.

The kitchen was hot where he sat at the table, moving a tin ashtray in slow circles with his fingers. If there was one thing Muss Drover could claim as practically guaranteed, it was wood for the stove. The certainty of heat. He would cut the trees in the thick forest behind his house and haul the stripped limbs out into the yard where he sawed into them. He kept the stove raging. The kitchen was stifling with heat, so that he sweated continuously. But he insisted that the heat was not for himself. It was for his frail mother, even though it never seemed to reach her room, leaking out through the gapped matchboard walls beyond the kitchen on the bottom floor.

Mother Drover was sleeping in the upstairs bedroom. Muss had brought her a biscuit and a cup of tea after arriving home. He had carried it up the stairs and, reaching the top landing, carefully turned for her room. She was cold where she lay back in the bed, staring at

Muss, her sappy eyes casually shifting down to watch the space beside him, her thin-fingered left hand dangling where it always was, over the edge of the bed, waiting for the touch of the mongrel's wet nose and quick insistent head.

Mother Drover did not say a word; the silence of the last few weeks, only biscuits and tea finding their way to her. And occasionally the cured fish that stung her mouth with its intensity of salt burning her cool lips. The old dry potatoes and no table butter. She sighed her usual rising sound as Muss helped her to sit up and back against the two pillows. A droplet of sweat dripped from his narrow nose as he looked closely at his mother with no words in him, before stepping away, moving from the room, but leaving the door open and briefly smiling back, wanting the heat to find its way into her room, frustrated by how the air here was always cool to the nose and the fingers.

Mother Drover raised the biscuit, holding the edge between her gums, and snapped off a piece. She quietly sucked it in her mouth until it turned to paste. Everything was mixed together now, what she remembered and the feeling of it turning soft in her mind, the spark and purpose of timely thought abandoning her. Raising the tea, she took a wet sip. It was hot and— when she swallowed— harsh, leaving a scalding trail. Moaning and stretching her neck for an instant, she laid the cup on the wooden tray across her lap and cracked loose another piece of biscuit. Her eyes studied the room and she grunted lowly and gently nodded to herself as if confirming suspicions she had held for decades. The house was growing old around her. Her son seldom spoke with her. He seemed afraid to talk. It was fear or shame. She could not strike a wedge between the two. She wondered about the tea, when it would turn watery, the same bag used for the third time. She sniffed the second biscuit, then placed it back on the tray with dislike. Slowly brushing the crumbs from the bosom of her nightdress, she stared at the off-white wallpaper with the tiny red roses and faded green stems; it was peeling away from the moulding at the ceiling, widening brown outlines of water stains flawing the surface. The flickering dimness of it witnessed by the light of three candles, one on her night table, one on the tin circle set atop her washstand, and the other— the third that was usually positioned on a small shelf beside the chest of drawers... the third— gone. It had burnt itself out and, with a brisk sudden shiver, Mother Drover sensed the darkness that was over her shoulders, out the window where the night sky hung low. It was brewing there, casually slipping in closer when the third flame had hissed out. Deceitful. It was always present. The darkness was always present, she informed herself. It was only the light that made it appear to be gone. But it was always present. Take away the light and what did you have? Close your eyes and where were you?

She stared at her husband Hoddy's washstand and dresser. One night she had woken to see Muss carrying the tilted washstand to the door, but lingering at the threshold, with the piece of furniture in his hands, looking off through the window as if paused by the clearing sight of the sky lightening or darkening— it was dusk, maybe dawn, and Mother Drover was sleeping across these borders, confusing them. Muss looked at her, but her lids were only open a crack and he was blind to the knowledge of what she saw, what she remembered. She wanted to tell him. The need was there, but it was quashed by a sense of finality, of things moving away from her, as if to utter such certainties would mean the absolute end of her. She could not help but sigh, and Muss returned the washstand to its place. What would he get for it, anyway? The merchant— Wil Normore— was a thief, though a kind thief, all the same, from what Mother Drover remembered. He would lend with one hand and steal with the other. This duplicity reminded her of the disparate exploits she had been through. She sighed again with the burden of such complete thoughts pressing down on her as if to drive her from her own body. She had watched her son open the drawers of the washstand, feeling the worn wood, the smoothness of the joints. Muss was thinking of his father, of the dovetailing and how the trees had been planed and cut to fit together as if they had been one artful thing all along, needing only the instruction of the old man's craft to embellish the almost obvious.

Mother Drover had nodded to herself in silence, knowing this for a fact. She lay quite still with her thin soft arms beneath the heavy quilts, and watched Muss brush his fingers over the wood. The sound of the stroking motion had made her blush, and she had felt the heat rising in her cheeks and the soft stirring in her thighs that came to her as if she were a young growing girl finding pleasure in the sight of something that crossed over the line from startling into thrilling. She knew there was something there, how her own son reminded her of her husband, how this act of intimacy was bearing them closer, and there was nothing she could do to cleave the unity. Remembering like this, she let her left hand hang over the side of the bed. The distance to the floor seemed well beyond her reach with the open air against her skin. She weakly bent her fingers back and forth.

"'ere mongr'l," she said to herself, speaking in a slow and distant manner, as if the dog were elsewhere now, curled and sleeping in a place where only mournful voices could find their way. Quietly moving her hand back and forth, "You 'member 'oddy, mongr'l. Me 'usband 'oddy. When I'd wipe the sawdust from y'r belly..." Mother Drover grunted, agreeing with herself. "You be sleep'n' in 'is shop. Sad-eyed dog." Raising her hand and sloppily wiping at her big nose, she pressed her lips together in grim appreciation of the thought. "All ya be want'n' was fur yer head ta be rub'd. Dat's all, me love. Dat's all ye be affer."

Muss opened the back door shortly after hearing the shotgun blasts, the sounds so close he could discern the vibrations against his fingers and against the bottoms of his feet. He drew a damp sleeve full across his face. Someone was hunting in the night, moving through the still black-snapping woods with a flashlight taped to the barrel of a shotgun, and firing at what moved through the bold beam of light. He could smell the gun powder, the quick burn of it in his nostrils, but then he caught a whiff of whatever had been shot cooking in a pot and realized that it was merely his imagination attempting to make a fool of him. He blew some air from his lips, driving away a droplet of sweat that hung there. Then he turned and lifted his own shotgun from the corner.

Pulling on his green wading rubbers, he trod off, through the field, to the edge of the woods. Turning back once, he surveyed the big square house and the impassive light that spilled through the back screen door, making him feel as if he was a stranger, disconnected from what he was inside himself, far away and plainly watching. The windows were black. He glanced up at his mother's room, wondering about her position in the bed, aware of her indifferent look and the heavy sense of resignation she nurtured for everything that had been taken away from her. It was a longing for such things, or for the death that would take what little remained, relieving her. He wondered if she had understood about the dog, always believing that if he kept things from her, then she would be saved from the stark inner thrust that struck out from such calamities. But he felt foolish thinking this way, realizing where he had come from and how his mother could see things by the way he moved and by the words he tried not to say, the silence sure to fill in the bearing of any unspeakable truth.

The woods were black when he faced them. He slid the flashlight button forward and the beam brightened the grass and brittle blueberry brush at his feet. He thought of hunting in daylight, but so many people shooting had become a dangerous proposition. Fewer hunters were out in the dark, and what animals remained were better found at night. Traps were useless; the animals caught there were snatched away by the hunters who roamed in sunlight, making money from the pelts that were whole and not sprayed with shotgun blast.

The branches ahead of him were white and grey and seemingly

hard and delicate the way they climbed away from themselves, narrower and greyer at the tips in the fullness of the beam, the tips stirring against the low black sky, reaching and almost touching. The sky's blackness beyond the light seemed to sway as Muss walked, the blackness shifting with his steps so that he stopped, steadying himself against this impression of misplacement. He waited, then moved, but paused again, listening.

Another shotgun blast echoed above the trees, crackling out over the distant water. There was no way of telling which direction it was coming from; the sound rose and flooded above the vast wilderness as he pictured his stunted body between the dense trees as if he were gazing down from the sky. Muss first believed that the sound was arriving from his left side, toward Blind Island, but when the next blast rushed down at him, he stared up, aiming his light at the sky. He thought of shooting to bring down the abiding presence, but what would flap screaming, tumbling, from above would certainly crush him and pin him beneath its dead weight.

Muss slowly levelled his head, guided the light down against the woods, the beam threading through the lattice of branches and dark brown tree trunks. The light scoped ahead, conveying his sight beyond himself. A rustling in the bushes to his left snagged his breath and he spun and tugged away the tightness of the trigger, the orange flame staining the air for an instant as the stock punched against his shoulder. The rush of smoke and the smell. The frenzied rustling on the ground; a sideways kicking of limbs through the dry grass and brush.

Hesitantly stepping nearer, Muss could see where the lead pellets had spread and lodged along the bottom of a tree, and further to the right, thrown beyond where the other lead had found its place, the limp carcass of what he believed to be a lynx. The shadowy darkness bewildered him, imposing a fear that the lynx might be something else, something unheard of and unstoppable lying there waiting to leap to its feet and swallow him as he took two steps and shot again, the bulk of the animal unmoving, only the slight meaty jolt of the lead scattering in its hide.

Muss kept the light targeted on the lynx's face, finding the tip of its tongue slightly out, its eyes open and staring on the sideways angle of where it had dropped. Touching the hide, he felt it was warm and thick and squeezed it between his fingers to appreciate the enduring heat. Then he pressed against the small wet holes he had made, wiping his fingers into the fur, then in the grass, sensing the coolness, the seemingly hollow impression of the earth.

Shots reverberated and held in the air. He flinched and ducked, holding himself and looking back. They were behind him now.

Untying the rope from where it was wrapped around his waist, he carefully pulled the length of it through his hands to hold it straight. He slipped one end beneath the lynx's wide furry throat, prodding it along the grass until he could feel its frayed tip coming out the other side, then tightly tied it around the lynx's neck. Tugging, he saw that the carcass would move without trouble, the head rising slightly, the weight of the body slipping forward. He dragged it behind him through the woods and out into the tall grassy clearing where he could hear himself breathing under the open night sky, then back into the sheltering woods that led to a narrow grove of trees. He forcefully shouldered through, snapping branches toward his house on the other side.

The back light was still on and dully brushing the grass. He dragged the lynx with both hands, his arms tiring, the shotgun shoved down one of his long green rubbers, the brutally hard tip of the barrel scraping the skin from his ankle. He had to keep pausing to straighten the shotgun. It was awkward, and when he arrived at the point behind the house, he pulled it out of his boot and let it fall to the grass, the cold thud of it sounding in his feet as he hauled with his shoulders and with the full length of his arms, until the lynx's head was resting on the back bottom stair. He tugged harder, the carcass sliding up one step, then another, and into the kitchen where Muss let its head drop onto the wooden floor, its eyes still open in the keen silence that followed, staring at the legs of the kitchen table. The tip of its tongue was pink and its ears were pointed and black at the peaks. Muss thought of its head as he stood there, folding open his hunting knife. He considered the weight of it and then he studied the paws. They reminded him of the furry hooves of the work horses he had seen coming up from the iron-ore mines on Blind Island when he was a boy, his father down in the big hole, red dust everywhere, on the people and on the horses and in the streets, the gritty abrasive taste of it in his mouth, making him think of spitting it away like the taste of fear that he recalled experiencing as a teenager when it was announced that the mines would be closed. It had been his family's only way of life and they had been cast away from it, their bodies like the literal roots of their generations torn from deep in the red earth where his father had been a mucker.

Those years ago, when he had heard the news, he had gone off at night, down to the stables where they sheltered the horses, deep in the mines. And in the dim light of the lamps with the dank animal smells trapped around him, he had killed one of the horses by thrusting a knife into the big vein in its throat. He had watched it die under the brighter light of his flashlight, its eyes shifting big and frightened as it dropped heavily to its knees and then struck the ground with its head as it went down with a blast of air from its huge nostrils. Muss had found a bucksaw and sawed through the front hooves of that horse and held them in his hands. The severing had felt insufferable, but lent him such strength through release. He was driven by a force working exclusively outside of his own body, having no relation to his person, a force that invented itself through the twisting of him and all of his family out of shape. It did not wait for reaction. It had no regard for petty physical or emotional replies. So he had taken one of the heavy hammers and spikes used to lay the track for the ore cars and nailed the horse's hooves to the front of the shaft entranceway. That would show them the ugliness of what they had done. And it would show them the strength and courage of his people.

Months later, Muss' family had moved across the water and settled, doing nothing, only lingering, cast out, his father's new bitter heritage: disheartened until death.

Muss kneeled before the lynx, took hold of its front paw. Tightening his grip on the knife handle, he vigorously worked his wrist to cut into the fur and through that paw, but the paw was too thick. He collected the short-handled axe from the back porch and whacked through the tendon and bone. Then— shifting in a duck-walk— he whacked through the other three— front and back. The lynx lay there, crippled, blood seeping in four black-red puddles that only went so far and then congealed. Muss lifted the two front paws, one in each hand, receiving the impression of their weight, pressing them together and in against his chest to fix them in place as he stepped out into the yard.

Remembering what he had forgotten, he laid the paws on the step and stomped back in for his hammer and four galvanized nails. He returned to the night air and drove a nail through each paw, two rows of two— one above the other— on the planking of the house. He considered it a sign for the hunters, notice that he was still alive and built of the steadfast daring required to cut down an animal of this calibre, carve it up and set the head on the stick that held the clothesline off the ground. Four-inch nails and blood trickling from the open ends of the paws to suggest that the house itself was somehow wounded, following the slow trails with his eyes. Following and following until they touched and sank into the ground, moving deeper, moving down, replenishing.

Turning and standing steady to face whatever presence was studying him from the forest, he needn't even say the punishing words that clung to him, hung around him in the cooling night air, like the heat misting from his unbearably hot kitchen.

The meal was more than he could eat. He saved what was left of the flank roast, storing it in the short round-edged refrigerator. He sat at the kitchen table, cutting up the last of the soft shrivelled turnip and carrots, glancing out the window as the sun came warm and orange-red through the evergreens. The colour never ceased to please him; the feel of it and the claim it made that the night had been driven back. The stew that he was making was mostly for his mother. She was fond of stew and he cut the meat into fine, small strands, so she could chew them with little effort.

It would be ready for breakfast when she woke from her sleep. He would let the meal simmer and wash the blood from the floor, wondering why he had not skinned and cut up the animal on the back lawn, wondering why he had needed to drag the carcass into his house. But knowing in himself why, being this close to such fierce and terrifying hunger, he understood it was a private act of testimony— the slicing open and tearing out of the thrust that had made this creature move. His hunger was like a lazy thing now, dulled for the time being by how he had filled himself with the complete taking of another.

Muss Drover had dropped the last of the vegetables into the pot and stoked the fire within the stove's iron belly before he sat back at the table, waiting to hear his mother knock the chunk of iron ore rock from her night table onto the floor above, the signal that she needed him.

Muss was sitting, waiting for the sound. Stirred so by anticipation, he was not startled by the sight of the dog, especially now, after the death of the lynx.

He tried to watch above the scorching rush of flame as he lit a cigarette stub, but he had to close his eyes against the heat, the intense light giving depth to the rutty unevenness of his face.

Snapping shut the Zippo casing, he stared through the window, saw the old beagle dragging slow along the path down the centre of the field, pausing on its shaky legs before coming slow again, its head bent down and to the side, its tongue hanging out, gasping, coughing dryly.

Muss stood from the table, smeared a palm across his face, over his brow, then wiped the sweat on his pants. He took a piece of raw meat from the refrigerator, and it was still warm in his hand, only chilly around the edges. He opened the back door, stepped down the stairs, taking his time to walk across the open field, along the rough overgrown path, until he was close to the dog and saw what it was dragging: the boulder at the end of the rope, the fur worn from the mongrel's bleeding throat, its tongue hanging out so that it lapped at the meat, lapping only for the wetness of it, not knowing hunger any more, only thirst. The strange smiling snout and the weakness and pain in its jaws, as if it had been laughing too much.

Muss lifted the rock, then scooped up the dog in his skinny arms. He carried the mongrel through the house, climbing the stairs and carefully treading into his mother's room. He waited there, holding the dog with its sad eyes staring up, watching Muss' face, appreciatively lifting its head to lick Muss full on the mouth with its tickling sandpapery tongue. Mother Drover was sleeping, her short grey hair thin and loose over the pillow, but her skin seeming fine and smooth despite her age.

Muss stood there breathing, the chill making the insides of his clothes extra cold. He set the dog down beside the bed but did not bother to untie the rock. He left the bloodied rope where it was around the mongrel's throat. Then he went out of the room, leaving the dog nervously sniffing at Mother Drover's hand.

Muss took his time treading down the stairs. He was thinking of the lynx's paws, saw them slashed loose and bounding minus body through the air. He caught a healthy whiff of the stew while watching his feet take the final stair. The smell itself invigorated him and he hurried along the wooden plank floor, then out the back door, moving without thought or effort to the place where he raised the hammer and worked to draw the four-inch nails from the lynx's paws, yanking on the hammer handle, pulling and jerking, until the galvanized points were plucked loose and— one by one— the furry clumps dropped onto the ground.

A soiled roll of string was collected from the kitchen drawer and he unwound a piece, used his unclean knife to cut through. Bending to retreive one paw, he wrapped the string around it and then tied a tight knot. He took the other end and secured it to the second paw. Dividing another length, he tied the third and fourth paws to either end, then raised their weight and swung them around his head, spinning the paws tentatively at first, then faster, hearing the swooshing sound breaking up the air, faster, he worked his arm and shoulder, investing great effort into making them bound at unbelievable speed, the swooshing sound almost a steady whir, he heard the stride and crashing of the paws through the forest brush as it bolted for its prey, seeing the lynx coming for him, its head down and watching, its mouth ripping open with a vicious feline cry. He spun the paws at resounding speed, his eyes squinting beneath the blur of fur that circled his head, the need to shout rising as the rush of attack and escape welled up inside him. He would make that animal cry. He opened his mouth to match the discord, but found only running, pouncing laughter galloping up. Despite himself, he yipped and shouted at once, the laughter like the striking of teeth.

Muss' mother heard the sound as she slowly woke, knowing by the laughter beyond her room that she should be smiling even before she felt the moist nose against her hand. She smelled something cooking and moved her fingers back and forth until the mongrel edged its head closer, pushing against her fingers, wanting the scratching of her fingernails, pleading with a nudge, then weakly dipping its muzzle to paw at its open mouth, and hack with one retching cough shivering through its body.

"Wha' dey done t'ya, mongrel?" asked Mother Drover, feebly lifting her grey head and edging toward the side of the mattress to peek a look. The sad eyes stared up to meet her gaze, urging her to lean out further and use both nimble hands to carefully undo the knot.

St. John's, 1991

Behind Glass

Morning sunlight softens and warms the living-room carpet. I move from the kitchen to the big window. The drapes are open on one side and I stand there in my underwear and a dirty t-shirt with paint stains along the front. I look down at the bowl of cereal balanced flat to my palm. I cannot see my fingers. They are beneath the bowl. My other hand dips the spoon in. I leave it resting there against the rim and lift my fingers to the window. I tap the glass with my fingernails and wonder what the air feels like outside.

Across the narrow street, an adolescent boy holds an axe high over his head. He brings it down with a vengeance. Chips of ice spray into the winter air. The boy is wearing an old down-filled jacket and jeans. His hair is short and matted with sweat. He moves up and down the street with the axe flashing and chipping. Spring is on its way. Things are melting.

I look to the spoon and grip it with my fingers. I am amazed by how simply my fingers perform their duty. Filling the spoon with flakes and milk, I lift it to my mouth and listen to the muffled sound of chewing. It seems almost distant. My jaw makes a solid cracking sound. I remember hearing that sound from my father's jaw when he ate. It meant something then, something durable and sturdy. I chew quickly and swallow, hoping my jaw will not make that sound again.

I stare at the flakes softening in the milk. I move them around, then look up to see a furry grey dog lying in the middle of the street. It has the face of a wolf and does not move for cars. It watches and stares, oblivious to danger. There are several puddles of water around the dog. The asphalt is streaked with white from road salt and there are tire tracks from the puddles, but they slowly fade and are gone.

A car pulls into my driveway to turn around. I feel a mild sense of violation. My property. My driveway. I lift the spoon and open my mouth. I slip the cool steel in, then slip it out. I chew as the car swerves back, straightens, then roars away.

Another car passes. I know that car: the big, white two-door with the blue roof. I see Miranda at the wheel. She doesn't look at me. Her eyes stare straight ahead, face blank and tense. She drives by fast.

I smile and tap the spoon against the window. Cool, thin metal tapping cool, thin glass. I like the sound. I tap again. I tap louder, then hold the spoon away from the window and dip it back into the bowl.

A man opens his door and glances up and down the street. He stands in his doorway in a loose grey t-shirt and baggy jeans. He usually stands in his window, but now he's out. His hair is grey and white. He flips the lid of his mailbox and looks in. Nothing. It's Sunday, but that doesn't stop him. He checks the mailbox two or three times a day. It doesn't matter what day— Monday, Wednesday, Saturday, Sunday. He looks anyway.

Finding nothing, he stares my way and nods. I lift the spoon and smile with a full mouth. I tap the glass. He tilts his head to the scaffolding in front of the house next door. The scaffolding's been there for months. Someone is painting the front of their house. I look up and see a cat lying on the top plank. Another stray cat sits on the asphalt and stares skyward. Two more strays prowl around the metal legs.

The cat on the plank is female, in heat. Sometimes, I hear the same gang of cats in my back yard. I hear their screams like a baby's cries from hell. I hear the sounds through my windows, slicing through the glass. I hear the female purring and pleading, and I hear the males fighting each other and shrieking for control.

I know Miranda's car will pass again. I wait. The man flips the lid of his mailbox, peers in, then steps into his house. I hear the muffled thud of his door closing. The grey dog slowly turns its head toward the sound. Then it watches a police car amble up and stop three doors away. Two policemen step out and stride to the door. The big one knocks. I barely hear the sound. The smaller one scans the street. The big one knocks again. They wait. The smaller one steps forward and knocks. I don't hear anything. The big cop looks at him as if he's crazy. No one answers. I see the curtain part an inch or two upstairs, then fall back into place.

There are people standing in their windows. They stand there day and night and watch the street. They watch now as the boy with the axe wanders by the policemen. The boy doesn't care about the policemen. He has something else in mind. He stops across the street from me and leans forward. He chops and chops as if hacking away at some despised image. The smaller policeman stares at the boy and shakes his head. His hat is too big for him. So is his jacket. His pants look okay, though. His shoes aren't bad, either.

The big one knocks. He knocks with big knuckles. I hear the dull sound vibrating through my window. The shorter one gawks my way. I raise the spoon and hold it level with my chest. The shorter one watches me. I wait. I shrug my shoulders. He looks away.

Stepping back into the police car, the big one glances at the boy. I eat my cereal. I taste and feel the flakes and milk in my mouth. I watch the policemen talking behind glass. Who knows what they're saying? Police things. Information. Good guys. Bad guys. Bang. Bang.

I wait, watching the dog lying there with its head up. It seems numbed to incidental matters of movement. It ignores everything— the boy, the police car rolling past, even the stray cats circling no more than ten feet away.

Miranda drives by. I smile. Her car slows. This time, she looks in at me. She stops the car in the middle of the street and stares. I watch her face behind the car window. Her lips move slightly.

I dip my spoon into the bowl without looking down. I move the flakes around in the milk. There is no sound. The flakes have gone soft. Then I lift the spoon and tap the window. I tap the glass twice. I tap louder. Then, I tap louder and louder.

The furry grey dog struggles to its feet. The dog is pregnant. Very pregnant. It moves to Miranda's car and sniffs the door. The dog is standing in a puddle. Miranda looks down and sees the dog. It dips its head and drinks from the puddle. It licks its snout, then licks some water from the car door. There is ice on the car roof. It is melting. It dribbles down the metal sides.

Miranda taps the car window and smiles at the dog. Her face softens as her lips move with kind words. The dog sniffs and Miranda looks toward me. I smile. Her smile freezes, then melts. She drives on. The dog turns to me. It stares accusingly.

The faces in the windows are watching. Some of them watch Miranda's car, others watch me. I wonder what they see. I wonder what they are thinking. I finish my cereal and walk away from the window. I sit on the couch and switch on the television. The morning news is playing. I leave the volume off. It's like I'm watching behind glass.

What's new? I ask myself. What's happening in the world?

I turn my head to the window. Nothing is moving outside. The faces are watching. I glance back to the television. Everything is moving there, moving in a strange and silent way.

I stare at the empty bowl on the coffee table. I don't remember putting it there. It's empty. It's empty and silent, like a picture. I move it to the other end of the coffee table. The telephone rings from its stand in the corner. It is loud and too close to me. I join my hands in my lap and stare at it.

Who could that be? I ask myself.

I wonder. The possibilities are limited. I wonder until it stops ringing. Then I look at the television. I lean forward and flick the screen with my finger.

Ping, ping.

I smile.

St. John's, 1989

Fitting Circles into Squares

for Sonia Dorothy Harvey

Jenny leans against the fence railing in her tight, worn denims. Her blonde hair, fastened in a ponytail by a string of rawhide, looks warm and soft the way it hangs down the centre of her back. Each of her pink-lobed ears is set with a tiny gold stud. I see them as she turns her head south and then north, contentedly taking in the vastness of our land as she smiles to herself. She is wearing her jean jacket with the corduroy collar, the wide dark outline of a stain still lingering across the back, slightly darker than the material, impossible to scrub away completely.

I find it hard to believe that almost a year has passed since the accident, but the sight of the stain brings memories nearer than I want them to be. Despite my offers to buy Jenny a new jacket, she will not let go of this one; it means something special to her, a trophy for which she has paid the price.

Shifting on her feet, Jenny leans awkwardly to the side, her left leg remaining rigid, a result of the car crash. It is early in the morning and the spring air is cool. Jenny has pulled on my pigskin gloves. She claps them together to hear the sound, then tilts back her head, watching the mist that she breathes from her rounded lips.

When Jenny turns her face in profile, it appears flatter. I see where her nose has been torn away, a black, clover-shaped opening in its place, like a hole blown through her face.

I have grown accustomed to the idea, just as one becomes familiar with the look of a friend or family member who removes their false teeth and continues speaking.

Jenny has a plastic nose that she fastens on with Prosaide adhesive. It is flesh-coloured and not very different from the one that God gave her. But she does not like to wear the false one when we are out here alone on the summer farm.

Back in the city, taking off her nose at night is an act of intimacy, and I feel my heart tightening, her face changing as she steps toward the bed, bending to kiss me, leaning nearer, the extra opening that I cannot keep my eyes from staring into.

The farm to the west of ours has been owned by Mr. Ward and his family for generations. Today he comes over to give us the bad news. His farm was on the market for such a long time that we'd completely dismissed the prospect of having to deal with new neighbours. Mr. Ward tells us that a couple, also from Toronto, fell in love with his farm on first sight.

"Young folks like you and you. The Bixels," he explains. "Expect a visit. They're looking to be friends with the world."

As a parting gift, Mr. Ward presents us with an old wooden tea box filled with antique hardware: stray knobs and latches that have been lying around his huge barn for decades. I have often— on casual visits to his farm— commented on the tragedy of not putting such wonderful hardware to use.

"You take whatever you want from the barn. Windows in there, old spare doors. But do it tomorrow before the works changes hands." With a somewhat troubled shake of his head, Mr. Ward confesses that he does not really care for the Bixels; they were the only ones willing to pay his stubbornly high asking price. They agreed immediately, without even haggling. Mr. Ward tells us he finds no value in this manner of doing business.

"No adventure that way," he says, his old shy eyes searching our faces for approval. We both give him quiet smiles.

I do not believe he wanted to sell the farm at all, posting the price so unreasonably high. In his mid-seventies, he has no family and plans on renting an apartment in an elderly support complex in Scarborough.

"Money's money, though," he proposes, shrugging his shoulders and wrinkling up his lips. "Those Bixels were willing. What can I say to that, except what I have to say now, in a sorry kind of way?" And with these final, practical words he bows slightly "goodbye" and backs away from us, turning and steadying himself, not able to look back.

"Take care," I call after him.

Mr. Ward does not reply. Instead, he raises his arms in the air and wiggles all his fingers.

"Goodbye, Mr. Ward," Jenny whispers, slipping her arm around my waist.

We glance over at the neighbouring farm. Like ours, it is without livestock or crop, most of the farms in the area having fallen victim to poor livestock and agricultural prices. Recently, the farms have become fashionable acquisitions, in vogue as costly summer retreats.

We stand on our front porch, watching until Mr. Ward finally makes his way up his long drive, nearing his home. He leans on the back of his pick-up truck, looking down at the dirt. Gently kicking at something, he stares a little longer, then strolls toward the cab and climbs in. Turning the truck around, he heads out his lane. We watch him pass along the road way up beyond our front fence. He toots his horn, but he does not look at us. We wave, and watch the dirt rise, then we turn in through our open front door and silently sit in the living room, watching each other for a while, unable to speak a single confident word.

The following day Jenny and I drive over in the pick-up and back in close to the barn's big double doors. We move quickly, feeling somewhat like thieves.

Even though Mr. Ward has granted us his permission, I cannot stop myself from glancing toward the distant road and feeling a manic stir of anxiety each time a car or truck passes. Jenny is less concerned.

She is more interested in the goods: the beautiful black ornate portrait frames, heavy hand-carved doors, and yards of elaborate millwork.

"Can you believe this?" she asks, affectionately touching an intricate pattern on one of the door panels as I lift it past her.

"Beautiful," I have to say, setting it against the hatch of our pick-up, then lifting the bottom end, sliding its weight up, then carefully level. "Unbelievable. They don't make anything that could come close to this now."

"I love it." Jenny smiles, watching as I shove the door all the way snug to the cab. Then she turns and stares up at the big old farmhouse. "Too bad we never had the money," she says regretfully, giving her head a slight shake.

"What for?" I wipe my bare arm across my brow and feel the sweat smearing warm and loose.

"To have it." She looks at me. "Just to make sure it stays the way it is."

"Dreamer," I tease, wandering back into the cool shadows of the barn. When I come out again, carrying a box of ancient horseshoes, I see that Jenny is still watching the house, backing away from it, limping, and staring toward the roof, shading her eyes from the early sun that turns the sky so fiercely blue.

"You're just..." she whispers at the house, waiting, bending to one side, considering its nature. "Always so... solid and always... always just... what?" she asks herself. Her brow tightens with the question, thinking.

A moment later, she slowly smiles and glances at me.

"It's lived through a lot," she quietly confides.

"And it's still here," I say, brushing my hands together to rub off the dirt, "kind of like someone I know."

The Bixels make their entrance the following day. They pull into their lane in a blue metallic jeep with light blue and silver stripes along the sides and park close to the door of their brick farmhouse.

Stepping out of the jeep, the couple is soon followed by two young boys, leaning forward from the back seats. The family spills around the land, a few toward the house, a few off across the grass, like a tin of marbles that has been softly overturned.

A little while later a yellow moving truck kicks up a wall of dust along the main road before taking its place behind our new neighbours' jeep.

Watching the van driver step down from his seat, I see him fitting on his gloves, then pull a latch at the rear of the truck; the sound of the huge door slides up on its runners. A second man soon joins the first from the other side of the truck and they both stare up into the wall of furniture and boxes that seems as if it has been compacted into the space. They wait a moment, one of them spitting off into the dirt, before Mrs. Bixel calls out, coming up behind them, pointing and nodding and talking.

The Bixels appear on our doorstep later in the afternoon. Mr. and Ms. stand on our front porch and introduce themselves, first by name, and then by profession. Mr. Bixel is a graphic designer and Ms. Peterson-Bixel is a marketing manager for a small-circulation specialty magazine that caters to high-income consumers of quality travel packages. This is how she explains it, interrupting her husband when he seems to get it wrong. Benjamin and Louise. They are interested in the country life. Her husband agrees.

Gesturing toward our front lawn where their two boys play, they tell us that these boys are named Lief and Dayv.

"It sure is quiet out here," Benjamin says to me, resting his shoulder against my door frame and smiling in a communal, appreciative way.

"Yes, definitely," I tell him, the words barely from my lips as I hear Jenny's uneven step moving down the stairs behind me. She pauses, detecting the sound of voices, then slowly, quietly reverses.

"We thought we'd just drop over and say hello," Louise offers, tilting a little to the side to catch a glimpse of whoever she heard on the stairs. "Maybe we came a little too late in the day. Understandable. Wasn't thinking. You kind of stop thinking out here." She smiles generously, her eyes scrunching shut as she turns her attention back to me.

"No, it's fine," I assure her. Unwilling to ask them in, I vie for a diversion. "Fine-looking boys," I say, filling in the brief patch of silence. I glance past them, nodding toward Lief and Dayv.

Benjamin says, "Lief is eight and Dayv is two years older, ten." The boys are bent close to the tall grass, studying something, then quickly glancing back at their parents. Dayv holds up the long white rubber sheath, then lets it drop, and, jarringly, I remember it from the night before— how I left it out there, forgetting to throw it away after Jenny had gone into the house to prepare a snack for us, leaving her jeans behind so I could watch her naked lower body as she stepped through the ankle-deep grass.

Dayv stands from his discovery and wipes his hands in his beige shorts while pushing Lief away from the spoils with the toe of his shiny-white sneaker.

"Get away from that," he says, steady command in his tone. "You know what you're not supposed to do." But Lief just glares up at his brother with challenging eyes.

The Bixels observe their boys, then follow Dayv's path as he comes running over, all the while anxiously watching his parents.

"There's a condom over there, Dad."

Benjamin Bixel smiles and nods. Louise Peterson-Bixel flushes red in her face and along the front of her neck, then makes a point of straightening the waist of her lace-trimmed country dress. It seems slightly too tight for her and she is noticeably uncomfortable.

"Go tell Lief to head on home," says Benjamin. "We'd best be doing that ourselves," he says, "chow time," sounding humorous in his new manner of talking.

I glance at my watch and think of the boneless skinless chicken filet on a plate in the refrigerator, waiting to be lightly battered and fried.

"Drop over sometime during the long weekend," Benjamin insists, sincerely dipping his head forward and nodding. "We'll be here until Monday afternoon. Until 12:45. We'll then be leaving for home. Monday, just after lunch. Back to the city grind." He makes an expression of distaste, his narrow face and small mouth seeming to shrink thinner. Then, he smiles, like it's all a joke. He beams, "So drop over."

"Sure," I agree. "Definitely."

Benjamin extends his hand and I shake it gladly. I am a touch more gentle with the grip I offer Louise.

"Come on, boys. Let's head for the fields." Benjamin sweeps his arm through the air, waving to Lief, who is crouched in the grass eight or nine feet from his previous location. He stands and scowls at his father, mother and brother who stroll away together, and, as he watches them, I realize that Lief is somewhat peculiar. Not only does his face seem much older than his years, he also appears to be watching from beyond ordinary life, staring in, as if not truly a part of the group that faultlessly wanders away from him, talking brightly amongst themselves.

"Come on, Lief," Dayv calls, turning to sweep his arm through the air, mimicking his father. The youngest Bixel stays put, then starts off dejectedly, all the while staring at the ground and moving his jaw from side to side. He spits into the grass, toward our fence, then glances over his shoulder, up into the top window of the house where I know Jenny is watching. It is our bedroom window and she often sits on the day bed that I built for her and stares across the flat fields that run on for miles, spotted by the occasional farmhouse, corral of Holsteins, tractor or white silo.

Lief walks at his own pace as the Bixels travel down our lane.

Making it out onto the main dirt road, the happy family ambles in the still-tree shade of the cooling day, while Lief hangs back, picking up one of the smaller rocks from the head of our drive, wiping it off and shining the hard surface with his spit before hurling it violently into the shadows of the trees just ahead of his sauntering family.

Jenny is in the small room off the kitchen, washing her jeans in the big white utility sink. She stands there in her silky underwear and I cannot help but watch her as she scrubs, how her movements make her round buttocks seem plumper and all the more pretty.

She is wearing a pink t-shirt with thin straps that rise up over her shoulders. Little pink bows adorn the front of each strap. I cannot see them now, but I remember because of how much I appreciate the top's snug fit.

I stand there without saying a word, admiring her long hair; the natural honey colour of it, a shade that many women try to duplicate with dye, impossibly. I watch her slender legs, the tendons stretching against the fairness of her skin. The scars of her left leg are thick and jagged, moving down her thigh to just below her kneecap. The scars are whiter than the rest of her skin and I think of the bodies of the various women I have known; how the skin of the olive or dark-skinned women is so much tighter and seemingly thicker and unsensual, while fair skin behaves more like the truer feminine ideal, being pliable and pale.

I wonder if this preference is something I have been taught, if I have been tricked into believing this, or is it an emotion that I actually feel? It is a tactile reality, a subtlety that my fingertips detect, and so I assume it to be an authentic measure. I carefully argue in my own mind, presenting chauvinistic viewpoints and then chastising myself in a deliberately dramatic manner.

Jenny glances over her shoulder and I see that she is wearing her nose. She smiles attractively, then returns to the task of scrubbing.

"Why don't you let me do that for you?" I ask. "I'm a better scrubber. Bigger muscles."

Jenny laughs in a you-better-watch-it way. "Women's work," she says, aspiring to sound serious.

"Then women should have bigger muscles."

"And men should wear the panties," she says. "I know what you're looking at, pervert-creep."

"How can I help it? Innate attraction. Simple biology." I step forward, press in close to her back, and gently touch my lips against the soft hair behind her ear, growling, "I'm a man, baby. So do me."

Jenny gasps indignantly and whirls around in my arms, "No! Really?! A man? Right here? A man of my very own!" Touching my face with her soapy hands, she holds my cheeks and kisses me with her tongue, her eyes closing immediately. She shifts closer, her clumsy left foot sounding against the hardwood flooring.

She kisses deeply and passionately, pressing her body against mine before suddenly withdrawing her affection. "Do we have to go over there?" she asks, her voice pouting, playing the little girl, but— as always— fully aware of her unfailing control.

"I think we should." Sliding my fingertips along her hips, I reach down inside her underwear, caressing the pliant skin along her hips, softly pinching and caressing.

"I hate meeting new people," she says, contently shutting her eyes again.

"But these people are so nice and absolutely wonderful." I lean back to take a look at her face. She is smiling, holding her lips tight as her high cheekbones rise, but she will not open her eyes.

"Oh, of course," she says.

"We'll just go for a second, okay?"

She pulls the smile away and shakes her head once. "Uh-uh. No way."

"I'll give you a special treat later."

Jenny's eyes are surprised when they open. Staring up at me, "Naughty, naughty," she says, tut-tutting and wagging a finger in front of my lips.

"Not nearly as naughty as what you're imagining, I bet."

She kisses me again with her hands behind my neck, sliding up into my hair, then down around my back. She moans and rolls her hips, bending her right knee and shifting to press harder against me, kissing and pressing, then briskly standing back, away, smiling mischievously.

"Okay," she says, "fine. Let's go now, then. If that's what you want."

"Not nice," I whisper with a sigh. "No, not nice at all."

"If you want me," she says, turning away and dipping her hands back into the sink, her body bending slightly, her arms working, "then you'd better learn to do as I say, mighty man."

"We'll wait 'til tomorrow. Okay? That'll give us lots of time to do other things. Is that okay with you, ma'am?"

"Now, you're getting the idea." She glances over her shoulder and nods with grim approval. "That's much better. You're a quick learner. At least I can say that about you."

Jenny pulls the hair away from her lips and watches me as she raises her cup of fennel tea. She takes a sip and smiles appreciatively at Ms. Peterson-Bixel.

"Tastes like licorice," Jenny says, trying to conceal her displeasure.

I know that she does not like licorice, it being a favourite of mine, so I attempt to save her from having to swallow the repelling flavour for the sake of politeness.

"I love licorice," I say, leaning from my wicker porch chair, abandoning my glass of lemonade, and extending my hand toward Jenny. "Can I have a taste?"

"You bet," Jenny insists, handing me the cup and saucer.

When I glance at Louise, I see that an extremely concerned expression has pulled her features taut. I assume that she is worried about the china, as it appears to be quite old and the passing of it back and forth like this does terrible damage to her peace of mind.

The transfer successfully complete, I settle back and sip the tea.

"Excellent." I smile.

"Go ahead," says Jenny, nodding and gesturing with her hand. "Finish it."

"Thanks. Are you certain, darling?"

"Yes, I'm a little too *hot* anyway." And she carefully winks at me.

I take another sip with my pinky finger stuck out so that it may hook whatever of importance might be passing close by. I assume that is the purpose of the pose. It cannot possibly serve any other function.

It is Louise's turn to give us her rendition of a polite smile. It is a fine one, too. Then she turns in her chair, staring out from the shade across the sunny back yard, seeing her husband and Dayv playing an awkward game of catch with their brand-spanking-new baseball gloves.

Lief is off to the side, tearing out handfuls of grass and patiently carrying each handful over to a pile close to our fence, as if making a huge nest near the dividing line, his own natural retreat along the border that will protect him from his people and the life they plan to live here.

I realize that I should be down there with Benjamin, bonding in the best of male ways, but I always find the company of women much more interesting. They tend to have a greater deal to express about a variety of people and topics. I am not interested in baseball scores and renovation work, which is the line of conversation that I am certain Benjamin will fall into should I step within six feet of him.

"Isn't it all so peaceful," Louise says with a glorious sigh.

I turn my attention back to the ladies and take another sip of tea.

"Yes." Jenny smiles again, shifting in her chair, her left leg straight out in front of her, her right knee bent slightly.

"It must take some getting used to," says Louise, glancing at Jenny's leg, but— I assume— referring to the tranquillity. "This morning Benjamin rose from bed and called to the birds to keep it down. It was 4:00 a.m. They made such a racket. Get it? It's so funny if you saw him do it."

I laugh briefly and lay my cup and saucer on the glass top of the wicker table. Louise quiets instantly and her eyes do not leave me until the china is safely set in place.

"Beautiful china," I observe, feeling that I must.

"Yes, we bought it from Old Time Antiques on Bloor. It cost a pretty penny."

At the sound of this, Jenny stands from her chair and walks off without saying a word. I think it a touch ignorant, but she abhors any mention of price with regard to beautiful objects.

The price is the curse that most beautiful things are forced to live with, she often says. *Possession. Displacement.* She stands on the edge of the veranda, close to the steps, and slips her hands into the back pockets of her jeans. Rocking stiffly on her heels, she flicks her hair back over her shoulders. It is loose and hanging long the way I like it. I can tell that she is watching Lief and I know that she has taken a liking to him immediately due to his difference from the others, his resolute and intriguing sense of oneness. She is aware of the disparity immediately and latches onto it. It is a trait that she possessed long before the accident, the collision seeming to jolt it closer to the surface, as if her sense of concern had broken through several inner barriers on impact, making it all the more pronounced in her mind. She is a very sympathetic soul, in a genuine way, without the slightest stain of malice or shallow pity.

"Hey," she calls to Lief, then stiffly takes the steps and limps across the grass toward him.

When I look at Louise again, I see that she is staring at me. Her plump lips smile in a girlish way, as if to say, "Now we are alone," and I know this is an act. Being a marketing manager for a magazine, adept (I suspect) at modifying her opinions to suit those of her varied clientele, she seems equally proficient at altering her appearance and mannerisms in an attempt to suit the way she believes she should appear in this region of the province.

"Jenny is very beautiful," she professes, but there is the gleam of a dark secret deep in her eyes, and her round face appears vaguely harrowing. "*Very* beautiful."

"Yes," I say.

Louise waits for more, as if I am expected to add something, propose a condition or two to her declaration, the admission of a glitch in Jenny's beauty. She wants to know about the plug of false flesh in the centre of my fiancee's face, the extension of plasticized skin that runs from her nose into her cheek, the outline attempting to meld with the natural shade of her flesh.

"Yes, she is. So absolutely beautiful." I regard Louise and my eyes are completely unchanged. The gleam of her secret is smothered by my sincerity and she straightens in her chair.

A few moments pass before she makes a comment. "Benjamin likes baseball," she blankly states, as if this is some consolation.

"Baseball's a good game," I tell her.

Casting her gaze at the house, she scales its height with her eyes, thoughtfully saying, "You should see the new look he's been designing."

"New look?"

"For the house, to make it more modern." She catches my eye, uncertain of how I will respond. "Combining the old with the new. Benjamin's a design genius when it comes to this sort of thing. He's known for it. Everywhere. His firm even receives calls from Europe, and you know how old their structures are over there."

"Just what the house needs," I say dryly, then stand, losing my patience. "I'll see what Jenny's up to." And I turn, wandering out toward where Jenny has knelt, talking with Lief.

"Hey," Benjamin calls cheerfully, when I am close. "See the Jays' game last night? What a game!"

I give him a thumbs up just as he expects, and he smiles and leans back, making a pitch that soars fifty or sixty feet past Dayv. When I look at Benjamin again, he is staring disapprovingly at his glove and squeezing it, then turning it over and studying the back of it, all the while skeptically shaking his head.

"New glove," he mutters.

I shrug my shoulders. "Can't trust 'em, eh?" I drift away from him, casually, trying to be discreet.

Benjamin shakes his head again and takes his glove off, pulling at the leather with both of his hands, trying to stretch it out of shape.

"Hi," I say, coming upon Jenny and Lief in their big nest of long green horizontal grass.

Jenny squints up. "Hi. What's up, sweetie?"

Lief does not say a word. He freezes, glares at my face with a look that pins me as an intruder. His eyes are those of a cornered animal. They dart at Jenny, not knowing what to do, before he reaches forward and rips off Jenny's nose. Springing up, he runs desperately through the tall grass, half-leaping, half-striding toward the distant grove of birch trees and evergreens until he has made it there. He rushes in, crouching against the wide trunks of two full trees, hiding between the lower branches, peering out.

Benjamin Bixel is overly apologetic and insists that he explain a few facts about Lief. But first, he instructs Lief to apologize to me (Jenny is upstairs, perhaps still crying, and will not come down). Benjamin then tells Lief— in his best stern voice— to return the nose. The boy takes it from the pocket of his shorts and hands it over to me with a sombre stare.

"Thank you," I say.

He frowns at the floor and nods. "It's just a nose," he scoffs. "I don't even want it."

"I think he should apologize to Jenny, too. More importantly." Benjamin glances around the kitchen and, shifting his thin body a little to the right, attempts to stare down the hallway.

"She's resting," I tell them. But Lief tears away and races through the hallway, scrambling up the stairs. I move after him, while turning to Benjamin with my palm raised as if to indicate that he stay right where he is. He gets the message and stops dead in his tracks.

"Lief," I call. "Jenny's asleep." But he is already at the top of the stairway when I step on the first stair. He wheels away with his hand gliding over the bannister, turning and racing toward the front of the house, toward the room where he, no doubt, saw Jenny standing in the window two days ago. He bursts through the door and turns for where I know Jenny is lying down. I hear his cry as he throws himself onto the bed.

When I arrive at the threshold, he is flat on top of Jenny, holding on for dear life and crying, pleading, "I'm suh suh sorry," through the tears, his chest heaving and collapsing with great child sobs. "I'm... suh suh sorry. I... didn't... hhhurt it. I just... huh huh held it. Only."

Jenny strokes the boy's hair and whispers, "Shhhh," while watching me with teary eyes. She bites her lip and tries not to sob.

Stepping toward her, I present her with her nose, but she just takes it from me with her free hand and lays it on the night table.

"It's okay," she says, staring down at Lief's face, and gently stroking his back. "Shhhh, honey, it's okay. Nothing's wrong now. Nothing's wrong."

I am told by Benjamin that Lief's real name is Bobby Hogan. (A very plain name, as Benjamin sees it.) The Bixels took Bobby-Lief into their household on a trial basis a little less than a year before and he has been nothing but trouble since the first day he arrived. He steals food from their kitchen and hordes it under his bed. In school, he steals other children's lunches even though his lunch is more than adequate. He lies constantly and is overtly mean, without justification, to his class-mates.

"What's there to do with him?" Benjamin asks, as if we are the oldest of friends. "We give him everything he wants. We're kind to him."

I sit across from Benjamin in the kitchen. Bobby-Lief is with Jenny. She instructed me to leave the boy alone with her for a while. That was twenty minutes ago and there has not been a sound from upstairs.

"I don't have any children," I tell him, feigning ignorance.

Benjamin laughs, as if to say, *You don't know what kind of fine torture you're missing.* And I decide— I do not like this man. I like him less and less by the moment.

"We wanted to do something for the world," he explains reason-ably, holding and watching the cup of coffee that I felt obliged to offer him. "Make a difference. Help one child who needed help. It would be good for him."

No, good for you, I want to say.

"But he's a handful, Bobby."

"Why do you call him Bobby, now?"

Benjamin looks at me, his eyes knowing nothing of what I mean to imply. He is not aware of the likelihood of his own wrongdoing. As far as he is concerned, he is a saint. He is the tortured one, martyring himself to the task of caring for this disturbed orphan boy.

"You called him Bobby."

"Yes, I guess I did."

"No longer worthy of the name you've given him?" It is a mistake to say this. Benjamin's face changes immediately, even though I have tried my best to hold my tone neutral.

Since offence is already taken, I decide to push a little further, go all the way. "Doesn't make the grade, in your orderly, sterile exist-ence?"

"I don't—"

"So he goes back, sent down to the lower ranks, like something... like someone demoted." I am holding back, keeping myself from cursing and physically removing Benjamin Bixel from my kitchen. "Is that it? Get out of my house."

Bixel uses his long fingers to push himself to his feet. He stands there next to the table and glances at the back door as if planning his escape. Then he looks at me with worried eyes.

"What about... Lief?" he carefully asks.

"We'll bring him over." My voice is hard and final and he knows better than to contest my words.

"He's mine," Bixel whispers, but his eyes are meek and he stares down at his suede desert shoes, perhaps understanding for a moment, perhaps feeling, but unable to recognize what could possibly be missing.

"I guess we were wrong to expect so much of ourselves," he whispers dramatically.

"Stupid, horrible dangerous people," Jenny says, gritting her teeth.

After dropping the boy back at the Bixels' farm, I decided to tell her the story of Bobby-Lief, and the details infuriate her. We walk along the road on our way back to our farmhouse.

"Just what a child with a bad self-image needs," she says angrily, "a name change, and on a trial basis. Fuck!" She shivers and paces ahead. Her arms pound against her sides and she makes a small lopsided jump that, despite the circumstances, appears somewhat comic.

"What did you two talk about for so long?" I ask. "Up in the bedroom."

Jenny glares at me, trying to calm down. "Nothing," she says. She rubs her face and I see the false skin along the side of her nose rising a touch. "We didn't say anything. He just lay in my arms and I understood him. He knew that I understood him. It was like that; so easy." Jenny bursts out crying. "Those pricks." I notice how she gently touches her nose, pressing it firmly back into place, while she weeps, "Why are people so goddamn cruel and stupid?"

A month later, we see that the Bixels have returned to their farm. We see them across the fields. We see Benjamin Bixel playing catch with Dayv and we see Ms. Peterson-Bixel sitting on her back porch sipping from an ancient china cup.

There is no sight of Bobby. There is no Lief. Lief is gone.

The next day, I hear a big truck arriving early in the morning. Glancing out our bedroom window, I discover that the truck is from a building supply company over in Whitby. A short while later, three workmen appear in a pick-up truck. They begin by building a neat square extension like a geometrical cube onto the side of the Bixels' house, facing our land. Over the next few weekends, the back porch is extended and a garage is built onto the other side. The house is no longer the house it was. It is changed: remodelled to fit a lifestyle it was never built for.

"They've made it so ugly," Jenny bitterly comments on one of our after-breakfast walks.

I cannot pass comment. I do not want to provoke her. It is a calm morning; still and pleasant, and I know that she has been thinking about Bobby. Her moody silences over the past several weeks could easily be attributed to thoughts of the child.

"Poor Bobby," she says, confirming my suspicions. She stares at the new shape of the house, watching it with hostility in her eyes as we pass. Then she darts a look down at the road and kicks a bunch of small grey rocks into the ditch.

"They gave him back," she says. "Those evil fucking monsters. Can you believe it? They gave him back, like... like..." She shakes her head and looks at me, helplessness straining her features. "Like something cheap and broken." Tears spill from her eyes. Angrily, she swipes them away, accidentally knocking loose her nose. She makes a mean face. "Oh, I hate them so much," she cries, ripping her nose from her face and hurling it onto the ground. "Jesus, I hate..."

"Come on," I tell her, glancing at the dirt that has clung to the back of her nose, lying there so useless and detached on the well-worn road. "It won't do any good."

"I'm allowed to hate them if I want. I can do that much."

I make an effort to pick up Jenny's nose, but she grabs my arm with force and holds it tightly, staring at me with a warning in her eyes, before the distant sound of a screen door flapping shut catches her attention. We both glance at the house at the exact same time. Louise and Benjamin Bixel move out onto the front lawn, having spotted us coming up the road. Mr. Bixel has one arm around young Dayv and he is smiling and calling to us in a friendly way. His wife stands by his other side in her short-sleeved country dress, her hair swirled up into a neat bun that makes her face even rounder, plainer.

Jenny tries her best to ignore them, but I must watch to see what happens next.

"Hey, neighbours," hollers Benjamin Bixel, sweeping his hand high above his head. "Good morning." His voice rises through the still summer heat, mingling with the quick clear chirpings of birds.

"Goooood moooorning," calls Louise Peterson-Bixel in a bright breezy sing-song. Her smile is genuine and full of uncomplicated pleasure. "What an absolutely beautiful day."

St. John's, 1990

Better Not Mind Nothing

The woman has purple half moons beneath her eyes and a plain, hard face that resembles a man's. Her skin is thick and porous with dark, narrow lines of dirt in the creases along her neck. Her jeans and jean jacket are brand-new blue. "Presents," she tells me with a raspy voice, winking and coughing. She says something else, but I can't make out the words.

"What?" I ask.

"You heard me," she says.

A short stout man stands beside her. His head is round, his hair cropped military-short. He has a wide mouth and large, gapped teeth. I keep my distance. He seems to want to bite someone, but instead he simply chuckles deep in his throat and pushes his chin forward, showing me his bottom teeth. Smiling, his tiny eyes disappear in puffy sacks.

"I never heard you," I say, moving in behind the counter to serve a young woman. I try my best to concentrate on punching in the items but the black-eyed woman is grumbling beneath her breath. I glance up and see that she's whispering to the man with the wide mouth. Wide Mouth listens gleefully. His fat chest throbs, pulsing with dull, machine-gun laughter.

"Thanks," I say, handing back the young girl's change. I bag the tampons, chocolate bars and toothpaste, then slide the parcel toward her. As she lifts the bag, her scrawny face goes red, then redder when I tell her, "Have a good night." The girl won't look at me. Black Eye and Wide Mouth watch her with interest. They follow her every step, sizing her up, until she's out the door.

"Wince says his brother had a piece of her." Black Eye tilts her head toward where the girl has left. "She's like that. Likes to take it." She makes a fist and slams it into her open palm.

I study Wince with clinical observation, but he doesn't seem to take offence. I try to imagine his family.

"Wince's brother doesn't look much like him." Black Eye laughs with an opened mouth. She lets her tongue hang out as if she is a dog. Her lips are chapped and her teeth are rotten and brittle-looking.

"No," says Wince, emphatically shaking his head. "No, he don't. And don't say he does. He's fucking ugly."

"Don't worry," I tell him, then stare up at the big clock straight ahead of me, on the wall at the rear of the magazine and greeting-card aisle.

"You going somewhere?" asks Black Eye, glancing over her shoulder and reading the time. "What time is that?" she asks.

"Getting off soon time, that's what."

"Go for a beer," says Wince. He squints meanly and shoves his lower jaw forward as if it's a threat.

"No." I shake my head. "I've been here since eight this morning. It's almost dark now. I'm going home."

"You should have a beer with us," says Black Eye. "You should do that." She straightens her back against the rack of chocolate Easter eggs, then leans forward, running her hands up and down over her jeans.

"What's your name?" asks Wince. "Tell us."

"Juke."

"What kind of stupid name is that?"

"I don't know," I say drumming my fingers on the counter top. "My name."

"It's a nice name, Juke," says Black Eye. She takes a few seconds to watch my hands, then traces the features of my face.

"Thanks," I say.

"Stupid name." Wince laughs in his chest, the sound and movement like an animal stuck in there trying to buck out. He sucks on his big bottom lip and chortles.

Black Eye gives him a serious face.

"Shut up," she says, "you brain-dead maggot."

"Fuck off," he says, laughing through rubbery lips, the sound more like a hiccup than anything else. Then he's instantly quiet as he watches an old man shuffle into the store. The old guy squints beneath the fluorescent lights. At the counter, he feebly drops a handful of change in front of me and points to a brand of cigarettes. I lift a packet, but he shakes his head and points to the next one. Gripping it, I hesitate, and he nods quickly, grunting and staring off into a distant, out-of-focus spot.

The old man lays his hand on the counter, covering the change. He does this without realizing, so I have to move his fingers to count out the quarters, then the dimes and a couple of nickels. I push the remaining silver and copper back at him and he raises his hand, suddenly startled.

"Plenty," I say.

He nods without changing expression and delicately takes out a gleaming dollar coin. He asks for an instant-win lottery ticket. I bend down and lift the lottery can out from under the counter. I lay a ticket next to his silver and coppers.

The old guy nods again and scoops the change into his palm, then dips his fingers into his pocket, letting the coins slip in. Wrapping the ticket around his pack of cigarettes, he pokes it into the deep pocket of his worn black raglan. Then he freezes. First, he gives me a sideways look, then he slowly peeks over his shoulder at Black Eye like he's the centre of some kind of set-up.

"What?" says Black Eye.

"Yeah, what?" snaps Wince. He bites on his bottom lip, holding back a chuckle and eyeing me.

Shrugging his shoulders, the old guy shuffles off.

Black Eye starts out to ask him for a cigarette, but she looks my way and stops.

"You got one?" she says to me, lifting her fingers, as if holding an invisible cigarette to her lips.

"Don't smoke."

Wince points at my face, "Don't ya." He laughs, struggles to say something else but can't get it out. His smile stretches the width of his entire face, his big, gapped teeth looking pointy.

"Shut up," says Black Eye

"Fuck off," hiccups Wince.

They both stare at me. I open a comic book and spread it across the counter, dip my eyes down to read. A few moments later I lean forward— elbows on the counter— to get a tighter view of the colours and small words.

"We're customers," says Wince. "Look at us."

I glance up, eyebrows raised.

"Don't mind him," says Black Eye. "You know." She winks. Wince's thick fingers twitch at his sides. His arms are straight and short and his fingers move as if scratching an itch in the air.

"I don't mind," I say.

"You better not," says Wince. "Better not mind nothing."

"He just said he don't mind," says Black Eye.

They look at each other and Black Eye leans to the side and kisses Wince's big lips.

"Let's go out back," she whispers, loud enough for me to hear. She shifts her eyes slyly my way and knows I heard her, meaning for it to be that way.

"You, too," she says.

"I'm working," I say, smiling with disappointment.

"Working," mimics Wince, trudging for the door. He gives me the finger. It is a quick, stabbing gesture, and the tip of his tongue pokes out between his lips.

"Work, nothing," says Black Eye, tracing the half-moon bruise beneath her left eye. She winks and lets her tongue hang out, bending it up and tilting back her head as if she's licking me.

"Tongue your little hole," she says.

"I got a wife," I say.

"Got a husband," says Black Eye and she coughs and swaggers off, following Wince through the door while she calls back, "Big fucking deal."

I check the clock, wishing I could speed its hands. Ten more minutes and I'm gone. My replacement— Cody— comes in four minutes later.

"You see those two outside?" says Cody, scrunching up his small face in disgust. He stands about five-six and moves fast. "God Almighty!" He stares at the ground and squints as if he's tasted something foul, like he wants to spit, like his tongue's sweating for it.

"They're friends of mine," I say. "They're waiting for me."

"Come off it, Juke. Man, oh, man."

"Watch what you're saying."

"You're joking, right?" He leans on the customer side of the counter with both hands flat. I consider his small fingers. What's he supposed to do with fingers that small? He looks at what I'm watching, then lifts his eyes back to me.

"The big ugly one had his hand down the other one's pants."

"She's a woman."

"The ugly one?"

"No, the other."

"I drove them off. Told them to scram or I'd call the cops."

"You could've got something off her."

"Christ!" His face goes super sour. "Yuk! Don't make me puke!"

"I'm heading home now. Those two'll be back later if you need a quick one."

"You're a sick man. Sick." Cody moves in behind the counter when I step out. I don't glance back at him. I know what he looks like standing there. He's totally in charge. His hands are solid on the counter and he's waiting patiently for a customer.

In the back room, I grab my leather jacket from the hook and lean close to the metal exit. I hear noises out there. When I pop the steel handle, the door opens a crack. Staring down the steps of the high wooden landing, I see a dark body lying face-down on a pile of battered cardboard boxes. It's Wince. When I shove open the door wider, the light pans out to give me a view of Black Eye lying motionless under Wince's lumpy body.

"Hit me," she says, spitting over his shoulder. "Stupid asshole."

Wince turns his head and looks up. The light catches his face like a big, fat moon. The smile is the widest I've seen yet and the teeth look twice as pointy in the half-light. His tiny eyes are gone, buried in happy puffy sacks.

I step out and close the door behind me. The scene goes black. I stand on the landing waiting for my eyes to redefine the images below me. It's chilly so I pull on my jacket and stick my hands in my pockets.

"It's dark again," says Wince, thickly chuckling. "Fucking all right. The store man's up there. Watching."

"Let him in," says Black Eye. Her voice is clear and calm as if nothing's happening to her. But Wince is starting to move faster, buckling the noise out of all those squashed up cardboard boxes.

"Hurry up," says Black Eye, listening past the frantic sounds for my approach. I step down into the black, shallow hole and see the glowing tip of a cigarette. Black Eye's smoking. She takes a deep draw— ash blistering redder— and slaps and punches Wince's quivering back.

"Come on," she says. "Come on. You got it in or what?"

"Don't know," Wince pants. "Hole's too big, drive a truck up there."

I take the steps slowly, loosely holding the wooden railing.

"Juke?" she calls quietly, with a clear passion that startles me.

"Right here," I say, the stench of garbage and urine rising to me. I take the final two steps and move beside them. The flat cardboard feels tricky and unstable beneath my boots. Kneeling in silence, I lift the cigarette from Black Eye's mouth and lean back, sitting on my heels.

"You don't smoke," laughs Black Eye, kicking one leg to free it from the tangle of jeans around her ankles.

I wave the glowing, orange tip in the air. A set of headlights crawls along the building across from us, growing brighter and larger, stretching, then dropping away.

"Car turning," I say.

"I hate this. Fuck!" She slaps at Wince, who's got his head pushed over her shoulder, grunting against the cardboard, "that's not it! You know what you're doing, or what?"

"Yeah," Wince grunts and chuckles uncertainly.

I wait for Black Eye to look at me again, then I set the filter between her lips. She takes a deep draw and in the dimness of the fire she sees how I am watching her.

"Juke," she says.

"Yeah?" I stare at her eyes as the smoke streams from her mouth.

"That's some pretty face you got there." And she smiles in a genuinely nice way, her upper lip rising so I can see her brown-edged gums.

"Thanks."

Wince moans loudly and his body pitches up and then settles while he gasps for breath.

"Get off," Black Eye groans, shoving him to the side.

"Next," she calls, her voice echoing out into the dark narrow streets of row houses behind the shop.

Wince stays where he's landed, his head away from us, his face hidden in the cardboard boxes while he laughs or cries.

"You getting on, or what?" Black Eye asks me. I set the cigarette between her lips again and watch the red tip blistering long and hot as she takes the deepest draw yet.

"I don't know."

"Well, fuck ya, then." She snatches the cigarette from me and stands, quickly pulling up her jeans, then works fast to do the zipper and button. Turning, she kicks Wince in the backs of his legs. "Stupid maggot." She stumbles out into the dense shadows of the parking lot, singing an old country and western song.

I listen as Black Eye's voice fades, feel my hands getting colder while I breathe in the crisp air. It's quiet for a minute or two until the sound of cardboard rumbling disturbs the stillness, as Wince rolls toward me and doesn't move again. He stays that way for quite some time and I stay there with him, my eyes fixed on his face while I listen to the night sounds of shrill voices and tire screeches.

"What're you looking at?" Wince finally asks, his voice dull and far away.

I shrug my shoulders, staring at him while he stares back.

"Shut up," he says, and doesn't say another word.

St. John's, 1989

The Deep End

for Janet

Eyes shut against punishing sunlight, the man sees regardless, behind his lids a brilliant pink. The blocking out of light proves nothing. Even this blind view of the sun forces his eyeballs to twitch, and so he rolls them back into his head, toward flickering red and darkness.

A musky scent is roused from his body. He is lying flat and senses the hard grass beneath the white sheet he has spread against his back. He imagines the empty swimming pool he could easily see if he simply raised his head and peered toward his toes.

The sound of a woman's voice moves high above him, distant as if through sleep:

"Hey?"

His eyes open to see, vision overwhelmed by the sun's furious tension; white and scalding and drawing away from itself. He squints and shades his eyes. Sluggishly, he turns his head and sights the apartment building hazily coming into view.

"Thanks," calls the voice, and he sees her tiny figure, waving, hears the slow rattle of keys as they tumble from above— steel jangling in weightless mixture— coming crazily slow. Palms carefully laid flat to the ground, he pushes up and sits, steadily in place, the keys diving faster now, breaking through to him. Bouncing onto the grass, they tumble and land askew in awkward, firm settlement.

When the man looks up again, the woman is gone. He leans to the side and reaches, lifts the ring of cool keys in his hand. Holding them, he lies back down. It is becoming more and more difficult to determine what he is capable of. Sweat glazes the skin beneath the hair on his legs, chest and arms. A wall of heat blazes and pushes against his face, drawing a luxurious sheen.

A mere week from now and his skin will have realized the perfect shade of bronze, but he is not certain if his will can endure the stillness.

The thought of moving his arms away from his sides, sliding them along the grass, up over his head, enters his mind, but the idea of doing so with his eyes shut disturbs him. His limbs should not move through the unseen air.

From far above, the sound of a heavy door closing; sound booms out through the marble corridor, expanding across the entire sky as if miles away, fleeing, yet solid in his ears.

He cannot stop imagining the keys falling, landing, bouncing, like a lunatic on a trampoline, tumbling off, broken. His hand tightens on the ring. A fist is made of his fingers, and the cut edges of the keys press their contours into his palm. He waits for the sound of something to click, perhaps a tongue (made heavy by the exhaustive tonnage of discourse and discovery) dropping away from the roof of its mouth, about to express precise comment.

The man stirs, desiring relief, simple physical compensation.

The keys descend as if through water, the water dissolving and each key tumbling free, something pulled out from under them. Thick fluidity drawn in reverse, soundlessly sucked away as they jangle against the ground.

He picks them up once, (dissolving) and then again. Falls back, blindly, lying down. He sits up, reaches, encloses, makes a fist of his fingers and thinks of what is opening in his palm: the imprint, the design, a lock clicking, the cumbersome tongue dropping from the roof of its mouth. His mind will not discharge the memory of action, and so he sighs and sits up.

One slow glance around the empty courtyard, the low shrubs bordering the large rectangular area, the beige buildings on all sides; rising high with walkways and balconies, the drained swimming pool that he has stood in at night and stared up from, as if truly— only now, from such depths— seeing out from himself. He sometimes fears to remain sedentary among the inspection of such stillness, believing this summer calm may settle nicely and, subsequently, demolish him with happiness— a shockingly mindless prospect.

When he stands, the short, thick blades of grass push between his toes, shifting and aligning with the spaces as he walks.

The rust-coloured tiles along the edge of the empty swimming pool are smooth and warm, like hardened clay baked and flatly polished. The pool is painted blue: the exact colour of the sky, its vacancy as compelling and eternal.

"Water," he tells himself, the thought so simple, "is all I need to float."

Sharply raising his arms above his head as if to dive, he holds the pose, but laughs instead of dipping, lowers his arms (subduing the threat) and, staring down at his toes, curls them up, then slowly allows them to straighten.

He thinks of stepping away, but thinking means very little alone, and so he turns, making it happen, and is noticeably pleased by his sense of brash accomplishment.

The keys still in hand, he tosses them over his shoulder and returns to his place, lies down on the damp crumpled sheet, closes his eyes, and listens, waiting, breathing twice, in, then out, until finally— the sound of metal shivering as the keys strike the concrete bottom of the pool. The man has come to believe in the need to extend beyond himself; policies of ascent, including the responsibility of coaxing humour from his austere thoughts. And so he laughs, but quietly, listening and carefully hearing the keys land, then fall again, settling with a jangling shiver that draws gooseflesh to his skin, rings of keys tumbling everywhere around him. The sky littered with metallic debris.

Rain?

He thinks not.

He thinks,

Deceit.

He thinks,

Click. The shape of the face determines practically everything.

Then comes the boom of the door opening and closing above him, sky-crashing orchestration of sound, before the understated solo— the tiny, uncertain, yet steady, voice:

"Sknaht."

He thinks

it forward,

"Thanks."

And again, opening his eyes, staring up, he turns his head slightly to see the woman's arm, waving strangely out of sync, before snapping straight. Hand extended over the railing, she leans as if tossing, her fingers stiff in wanting, waiting for the keys to fly to her.

Fuengirola, 1990

The Broken Earth

The baby's first three teeth grew out black and rotted and she suffered greatly and then died with a screech. The last time Darry Mercer saw her alive she was lying in the spruce slat crate in the corner beside the wood stove. That had been shortly after the baby bit him, her jaws turned strong in her savage lashings against death.

Darry was telling the story to a thin grey-haired man standing beside him in Tommy's and he was explaining carefully, sweeping his arm along the bar to show the uneven marks of the teeth, and loosely tilting his head to look at the man to see that what he was saying was being followed. He explained again, then again halfway through, forgetting and remembering at once. Telling it with greater urgency as if to force the memory into a shape that would make itself plain and recognized, not only by the thin man with the grey hair who did not seem to be listening, but also by the woman with the stringy black hair who stared at the smoke languidly rising from the cigarette she had just crushed out, then crankily shoved the glass ashtray away from her beer bottle, all the while nodding at any words offered her.

"What're you saying?" the thin grey-haired man finally asked, staring at Darry with an irritated expression. The man was breathing heavily through his nostrils when he tilted back his beer bottle and laid the empty on the bar, signalling to Tommy that he was off.

"Right," Tommy said, retrieving the empty and slipping it into the case beneath the bar. "How you doing?" he asked, facing Darry squarely and watching his eyes in the way he had learned to watch a man's eyes from tending bar for twenty years.

Pointing sloppily with one finger, Darry showed Tommy the details of the teeth marks and tried to explain, but Tommy frowned and shook his head at the mishmashed slur of words.

"In a racket?" Tommy asked, leaning with both elbows on the other side of the bar. "Shocking when a man's got to bite."

Darry put up his wavering fist, concentrating to hold it surprisingly steady, and squeezed it tighter and tighter until tears popped from his eyes.

It was summertime but the night air was cold. It woke him shortly after midnight and he did not know where he was. The ground beneath him seemed wet, although it wasn't, only the cool hint of dampness. One of his arms was stiff and, trying to stand, he worked it loose to brace it against the building at his left.

Steadying himself on his feet, he stared ahead to the shallow gravel strip where cars and pick-ups were parked. He heard music sounding from behind the wall, live music from a band, and he knew then that he was outside Tommy's and everything came back to him in a rush, whirling through Tommy's and further back along the highway toward Cutland Junction through the community and into the back road between the trees where his shack was standing and Leanne and the dead baby. The dead baby. That was where his thoughts stopped, struck brick, and the pain cut him through his heart and up into the centre of his head.

There was only the idea of moving that offered any clue to comfort and so he stepped off, away from the unsteady space that he occupied, toward the front of the building where he waited and then went inside, heading to his left to enter the washroom.

Standing over the sink, he stared at his face in the mirror, then lifted his hand to wipe a smudge from his cheek, but his hand was black and he shivered at the sight of it, a pain in the back of his neck working its way down his spine in a weakening rush.

He glanced over at a big man pissing in the urinal, then tried washing his hands, taking advantage of the running water. Turning the tap, the rush of sloppy-wet flickering seemed to undam his thoughts and again he pictured Leanne back in Cutland Junction, the shack with the piece of scrap panelling over the door hole, the hum of the generator powering the single bulb hanging from the ceiling.

Darry heard the door closing on its spring. The big man had gone out. Checking his pockets for money, he found that he was broke. A boom sounded from beyond the door, the band starting up after the break, the drummer testing his bass drum, pumping the pedal with his foot.

Out in the main area two pool tables were occupied by men he did not know. The music had begun and he could see a dim crowd of people dancing in the adjoining hall through the opened double doors. When he looked toward the bar, he saw the man named Tommy watching him carefully, glancing up from a conversation he was having with a group of new people who had come to fill the bar.

It was a long walk back to the Junction. Darry thought it might be time to start that way. Pushing out the door, he felt the fresh night air against his hands and face, and sensed the stillness as something he must step forcefully through to dislodge the calm of what was straining to touch him.

The woman who picked him up was driving a new maroon van. She smiled at him when he stepped up into the seat.

"Where are you going?" she asked, waiting for him to shut the door before pulling back out onto the road.

"Cutland Junction," he said, eyeing her cigarette burning in the ashtray and the fresh pack lying on the black moulded plastic between them.

"Where's that?"

He looked at her and wondered what she was doing.

"Up there." He pointed ahead to nowhere in particular, then pressed his oily black bangs back over his forehead with the flat of his palm.

"Oh." The woman smiled and gently lifted her cigarette from the ashtray, put it to her lips and took a draw like a moist kiss. "You tell me when to turn." She smiled at him and her cheeks rose, giving her an easy-going pretty look that appealed to Darry, making him wish for other things, other lives, his heart sinking through his gut and snagging there to swell bigger.

He nodded, noticed the lipstick on the white filter as the woman set her cigarette back on the little metal ledge.

"You smoke?" she asked, watching the dark road that stretched ahead of them.

"Yeah."

The woman's eyes brightened when she peeked at him, a strip of brightness sweeping across her face as a car approached from the other direction and passed them. With thumb and forefinger, she touched a medallion hanging from a silver chain against the straight line of her dress at her neck. Darry stared there and saw the beginning groove of cleavage. It was an elegant dress, made of deep purple material. Velvet. Darry looked at her ears, squinting at the earrings with the same design as the medallion that trembled with the motions of the van.

"Have one," the woman said, raising the cigarette box, glancing at it, then back at the road.

Darry took one while the woman reached forward and pressed in the lighter.

"I'd like to see where you live," she said without regarding him, her voice implying something he did not quite understand.

The lighter popped out and he raised the orange rings to the tip and inhaled.

"Where you from?" he asked, the first breath of smoke in his nostrils.

She met his eyes and a slow familiar smile curved her lips. "Why? Do you think that matters?"

Darry licked his lips and took another draw, deciding to ignore her. That would seem the best thing to do, until he got where he was going.

The woman's hand reached for the radio, her slim fingers switching on the dial. She adjusted the volume so the sound of the peaceful music was extremely low. Considering Darry, her eyes narrowed as if these precise strums and strokes and toots of instruments were all that was needed to reveal this simple connection, this artful flow of music making things so very easy for him. Easy. Joyous. A celebration of life between them if he would only listen, and hear.

"Here," Darry said, tilting his chin up, casting his thinking ahead to snag on Leanne and what she was doing now. Maybe sleeping. Maybe awake and staring back into the pictures in her head of what she had lost.

The woman slowed the van and turned the steering wheel through her fingers, veering off the highway and travelling along the asphalt that soon turned to gravel.

"Far in," Darry said, snuffing out the butt of his cigarette in the ashtray.

"Good." The woman smiled again. "Don't worry. It's okay."

They sat in the van through minutes of silence, the black green spruce to either side of them brightened for instants, sweeping shadows giving depth to the density of the wilderness but helpless to define anything of the midnight black immensity of the sky. They passed through the still community, the newer houses up front, rectangular bungalows, and then the summer cabins, before the penitentiary came into view.

"You sure you're not from in there?" the woman asked, nodding at the high grey walls and the lit tower with the lone guard appearing so small as he rose from a chair to his feet. "You're not going to hurt me, are you?"

"No."

The woman laughed out a light breath at the thrust of Darry's serious reply. Her expression became concerned, but she was forcing it, as if not wanting to offend her passenger.

Gradually, the road turned narrower and only an occasional

structure came into view, with car wrecks, rusted refrigerators on their backs, tires and heaps of metal debris in the occasional yard. The van passed a dead animal tossed over on the side of the road, and then— half a kilometre further along— another seemingly shapeless animal, more on the road than off.

"Is that how you treat your pets out here?"

Darry shrugged.

"I'd never have known." The woman laughed lightly again, enjoying herself in a way that troubled Darry.

As if sensing his discomfort, the woman thought it appropriate to swiftly offer, "Would you like a drink?"

"I've got a wife here."

"That's okay." The woman winked and reached back with her right arm, to a box from which she lifted a bottle. "Is she pretty?" she asked, knowingly, breaking the seal and unscrewing the black cap. She enjoyed a long swallow from the bottle and blew out breath when she finished, handing the bottle over and licking her lips. "Yum."

"Yes," Darry said, taking it and studying the label printed in gold and black, the strange shape of the bottle. He tried a gulp and the liquor was smooth and stinging at the same time, the sting not so bad. He took another swallow and it was sweeter and he handed it back to the woman.

"I'm not here for you. You're almost something to me, but you're just a man." The woman paused to switch off the music, making her voice clearer, more plainly understood in the hollow of the van. "You can look after yourself, not ever growing anything inside. Right? Men don't really need women. They don't have that needy space."

Darry nodded, "Yeah," and stared through the windshield, the fumes of the alcohol still in his throat, making him want for more, its burning sterility clearing a place in his mind that knew of nothing but willful possibility.

"That's very good bourbon," she said. "If you like bourbon, that is."

"It's okay," he said.

The van passed his shack and he watched it as they went by, not saying a word, not seeing any colour of light in there.

"That was it, wasn't it?"

"No."

"Come on, now. Do you think I wouldn't know?" The woman handed him the bottle and quickly swerved over to the side of the road, turned off the engine and shut down the headlights, then faced him with her hands on her lap. She gazed at his lips, then directly at his eyes, and smiled quietly, as if readying herself to say something, to explain the specifics of a delicate situation, but then giving a slight shake of her head, deciding against it.

"You don't know what's in there, do you?" She set her gaze on his arm.

"Where."

"In there." Eyebrows knitted, she nodded at his arm, the one that had been bitten by the baby. "Who's in there."

Darry took hold of his arm with his other hand and felt the hurt of the wound as a place outside himself, as if he was holding the entire country with its day and with its night but more with its night clamped beneath his fingers.

"What's the matter?" she asked him, not merely looking at his eyes now, but searching them.

"What're you after?"

"I want to see my..." She paused and grinned through closed lips, then winked mischievously at him. "Oh, almost. Almost too soon. I want to see your wife."

"Why?"

"I want to see your house."

"Why?" Darry slapped the bottle back at her without taking another drink, the liquid sloshing around.

Shaken by his forceful gesture, the woman wasted no time in taking another long swallow from the bottle, her eyes watching him with brilliant fear and acceptance. Then her fingers scrambled to open her door and she stepped down.

"Your hands," she said, when she heard him coming behind her in the darkness, his footsteps sifting along the gravel shoulder of the road. She tossed the bottle to tumble and clink through the trees. "Your filthy black hands."

Leanne sat at the table beneath the window, watching out, barely seeing the two figures coming across the yard in the darkness, but hearing them. She had turned off the generator hours before and sat with the silence and black misunderstanding to accept it as part of her body melding through. Comfort there in the blind holding of her head with both hands the way she had cradled herself as if preventing her grief-struck head from dropping off. "The weight of it," she mourned without thought, only the exactless swell as one idea, whispering aloud, "Sweet Jesus," hearing the footsteps closer and then the closer noises, too. Someone touching the shack, hands shifting the panelling on the door hole out of place.

Darry stepped in, the woman finding the decency to wait behind him, only staring in at the small black space that seemed to belong so exclusively to Leanne, a walled hovel, a box of darkness, holding back the slow nocturnal stirrings of life rising from nests and burrows so skilfully set in the woods surrounding them.

"I knew there was something here," the woman said. "I just knew it. Oh, God." She stood shivering, staring at Leanne's still figure sitting in a chair, weeping at the words the woman had just spoken. "I'll gather it. I know I'll gather what I was after."

"My baby," Leanne softly cried.

Darry stepped over to the crate and stared down.

"It died," he wanted to say, but he had thrown away the words too many times and could not find them in him.

The woman moved over by his side and bent to the crate. "You look around long enough you're sure to find what you need most. Something tucked away somewhere. A mystery, maybe the mystery, my mystery almost solved." Reaching into the crate, the woman lifted out the baby and turned to regard Leanne, saying, "She's not dead," while holding the baby girl tightly to her shoulder, one hand against its narrow back, the other against its small black-haired head, fitting so perfectly. "Look at me, she's not dead."

Leanne sobbed fiercely, knowing differently, her head dropping weakly into her hands, holding on against the stormy blur of grief like billowing grey clouds moved by sky-high wind.

"You a doctor?" Darry asked, the faintest shock of promise in his dull voice.

The woman smiled tenderly at him without speaking, the three of them reduced to nothing more than shadowed outlines in the darkness, with only the dimmest suggestion of light along the sides of their faces coming down from the muted sky and in through the window.

"You bury this child and she'll never be dead."

"Noooo," Leanne sobbed and weakly reached up for the baby with both trembling arms, but the woman would not give her over.

"We're buried here now," the woman said. "Crawl into the grave like this. Deep in here. So deep." She gazed around the shack with stark delight and wonder, a tiny pearl of spittle against her lower lip. "Alive." She dabbed it away with her tongue and cautiously swallowed.

Leanne leapt up and grabbed the baby from the woman with such ferocity that Darry backed away, the side of his right leg striking the cold metal of the woodstove.

"Please be careful," the woman said, worriedly touching her hands against each other.

"Get out!" Leanne screamed, gnashing her teeth. "Get out, get out!"

The woman slowly stepped in reverse, hesitantly toward the door. "She's not dead. She's getting better." Then she turned and left them, her words still whole in the shack, "So much better now that I've gathered her up."

A few minutes later, listening beyond Leanne's quiet sobs, Darry heard an engine start and tires rolling over gravel, coming closer to pass. Two quick toots of a horn.

Leanne held the baby girl in her arms and whispered, "Shush, shush, shush," rocking back and forth and breathing into the flesh that seemed made warmer now by her own anger and heat and rage. Rocking back and forth to calm the death away. Back and forth to connect with the spill of continuance, to coax the end to its beginning again and leap into that space, have it take her, sweep her along, like a lovely river.

Without further word, Darry went outside and dug a hole in the moonless night ground and he came back in for the body that, once loosened from Leanne, trailed away from the growing sobs of its mother to be carried out into dank sweet air, footsteps only in Darry's head until he heard a faint trickling onto the ground and felt a warmness against his right hand. Fluid running out of the baby. Warm fluid, followed by a tiny cough.

"Leanne," Darry called hoarsely, turning back to face the cabin, anxiously calling again, "Leanne."

But Leanne would not move from the table. Head slumped

forward, she could not find the strength to believe in anything any more, not in sound or in action or commands from one familiar body to another. Only weight, permanence. Rock in a bag into water with no bottom. Limblessly alone as one and sinking.

"Leanne," Darry insisted, glancing at the fresh hole he had dug, the gentle sound of clay slipping, relieved now from the mistake he had come so close to making, his eyes fixed on the baby's twitching lips, then meeting with the broken earth as he flinched with fright to see the vague image of the woman standing still behind the open hole that gave its rich smell up to them.

"She's just crossing over," the woman whispered, taking one step forward. She stumbled into the thigh-deep grave with a grunt and stood there, lodged, wishing to rise. "You look around long enough," she pleaded when Darry stepped toward her to watch her sink without protest into the soft clay, then vanish with a mouthful of head-deep words, "you're sure to gather up what you need most."

Then only the nightness of the broken earth and the black-toothed baby cooing in his arms. Leanne's white eyes staring out from the darkness of the shack behind him, her fingertips curved along the door frame in the vague blue-tinted-black light, holding there to face everything exactly as it had been.

Burnt Head, 1993

Arrow and Heart Tattoo

I

From across the street, I can see a woman neatly dressing in her living-room window. Her actions are deliberate and graceful as she bends forward slightly to step into her skirt. One pale leg, and then the other. She slips the fabric up over her naked hips, then carefully guides the zipper. The length of her brown hair is combed back from her forehead and falls naturally. With a sweep of both hands she flicks it over her shoulders and becomes preoccupied with the intensely delicate task of buttoning her blouse. Her fingers are nimble and the muscles in her face stir slightly in concentration.

My bathroom window is on the second storey and level with my chest. I stand behind its curtainless pane, watching the girl, faithfully, admiring each gorgeous action. To the right of this bathroom is my bedroom, offering a larger window positioned just above the heater and rising toward the ceiling. I rarely move from room to room. Once in place, I wait until it is time to alternate roles. As night slowly settles, I step into my bedroom and stand behind the larger window. Then it is my turn to declare myself, to disclose my body in a way that will reward her for her own sensual revelations.

For the past twelve mornings— since her arrival— she has purposely dressed and undressed for me, and sat before the window. She is in her late twenties and wears long skirts and silky pastel blouses, or fine dresses pleated down the front. They are fashioned with rounded collars, buttoned high to accentuate her attractive face. Although good-natured and friendly in appearance, she does not venture beyond her front door. This shyness intrigues and consoles me at once. I translate her reclusiveness as a gesture of her utter devotion to me. Although strangers, we have somehow linked visions, the impersonal nature of our distance making the intimacy of disrobing all the more passionate and profound. Free of personal trivialities that often plague male-female interactions, our longing is purified.

Occasionally, the girl will stand and move away from the window. Her absence lasts no more than ten or twenty minutes before she returns to attentively sit and stare.

She stares at me.

At first her gaze seemed alarming, each elegant blink a sensual punctuation. Without warning, she will smile and glance at the ground, as if blushing, her features slackening with a look of yearning that unsettles my pulse.

I stand in breathless expectation. Plainly, she can see me. There is no reluctance, no sign of hesitation. The street is old and narrow with only a thin asphalt fronting before each row house. Sidewalks have not been laid. Only a chipped concrete curb runs flush where the fronting meets the street. At this range, I sometimes find myself whispering aloud. Her boldness draws me closer and I lean forward, my palms against the glass, the pane holding me in place.

I whisper— and it frightens me at times— "Come over. Come here." Our distance, although seemingly quite minimal, is vaster than imaginable. I am tempted to open the window, but I must restrain myself. The simple act of opening might startle her toward a more complex realization.

The girl bends her head to a sound in the street. A car with a damaged muffler rumbles into a space in front of her house. The driver— a man with long, thin hair and a bushy beard— swings out his legs and sits still, staring down at his boots. They are black and shiny and seem to interest him immensely. His lips move for several moments before he claps his hands together and squeezes them into one double-sized fist. Gripping the door frame, he grunts a shout as he pulls himself to his feet. His hands move around the waist of his jeans, tucking in his black t-shirt with a silver metallic skull imprinted across the front. The skull has red eyes and is smiling treacherously at the words spelled beneath its bony chin. The letters read: "Give me head until I'm dead." The man stomps his boots and straightens the Harley-shaped buckle beneath his stomach. His heavy arms sway as he confidently strides toward the girl's door. He knocks with unmistakable intention, his chunky face staring up the road.

The girl suddenly stands, cautiously drifting back from the window. Slipping away from the light, her face becomes shadowed in the dim recess of the living room. Her eyelids stutter. She nibbles her bottom lip.

The man steps up and knocks again, steps back. The girl lifts a hand to gently lay it against the space between her breasts.

Pacing back further, the man strains to look up at the girl's window, then— to my astonishment— he turns his thick neck to stare at me, behind my bathroom window. I stumble in reverse as if punched, duck down and move to the side of the pane, edge in close to the wall without stealing a glance. My imagination scrambles for possibilities. What will he do to the girl? What has he already done? Does he know about us?

I hear the pounding of his fist against her door, sense it in my wall, and I edge close to the glass to peer out. The girl's door has just opened. The dark landing and the faint rise of a stairway are visible. I turn my eyes toward her window to see the man shoving the girl back into the room, then seizing her long hair, pulling back her head, clutching her throat. She does not say a word. She does not struggle. Her face cringes as he rips the front of her pale blue blouse. My breath tightens as the couple falls back against the far wall and I can see them only as grey figures. The man is kissing the girl, his image blocking my view of her before he reels away from his victim and briskly moves for the big window. Glaring straight at me, he lifts both tattooed arms above his head, gathering the curtains in his fists. He yanks them shut.

I turn and stare down into the toilet. The water is clear and I am lost for a moment, imagining outbursts: the begging sobs of the girl, the harsh punching voice of the man. I turn for the sink and twist on both taps so the water rushes out, drowning these sounds that gush in a current all their own.

Minutes later, in the midst of humming to myself, I hear an engine start. Palms flat to the wall, I peek through the window's closest edge to see a clouding haze of blue smoke. A child— naked except for her white and pink heart-patterned underwear— stands in the centre of the road, blankly watching the rusty car. Her hair is a clot of dirty blonde curls and her nipples are strangely swollen, as if from supping. A tiny finger picks at her nose, curling and probing deeper. She inhales the smoke. I watch her chest rise, her belly fill with effort. The man waves at the young girl, rolling down his window. He wiggles his fingers. The child stumbles backward. Sucking her finger, she screams at him and runs off.

The car's front fender is painted grey, the remaining hulk dark green. Flimsy fragments of rust shiver as the man roars the engine. He stomps the accelerator while the car is parked. The sound vibrates like the bellow of a giant. He is shouting her name like this. He is commanding and punishing at once. *Next time*, growls the engine, *next fucking time*. With one final clatter, the sound subsides as the transmission clicks down into drive.

For the remainder of the day, I do not see the girl. Despite her absence, I stand by the window and watch the street. A postal truck delivers a cylindrical tube to a house three doors down. A cable-television van with a star painted on its side passes below. A young woman in a pink leather jacket hurries by. Her clipped hair is short and raspberry-coloured. Discarded litter— wrappers and bits of newspaper— swirl around her low pink boots as she lifts a beer bottle from beneath her jacket and tilts it back, drinking as she walks. At the end of the street, a second girl calls to her. They jubilantly embrace, join arms and skip off, jaunting around the corner. I must stop my mind from inventing situations. I want so desperately to hypothesize about the leather girl's past; her harsh banal breeding, her materialistic beliefs, but particularly— and I must coerce myself away from these considerations— the antics of her derelict sexuality.

With hands clutching the window framing, I close my eyes and wish for the appearance of the girl across the street. I need her curtains to open. Memory replays the gestures of her body: the gradual disrobing, casting the incidents in a subtler light, revealing her pale skin with slower momentum. When I hungrily open my eyes, the drapes have been parted, but the girl is not there. The street is darkening and lamplight is vaguely discernible in her window. I wonder about her injuries and what the man expects to wrench from her.

Soon, she will be dressing for bed, slipping her pink cotton nightdress over her head and intricately drawing down her white panties, leaning sideways to pull them from one foot, then the other, coaxing the silky material away from her ticklish toes.

I step from the bathroom and into my bedroom. The house is divided into two apartments: one downstairs, the other upstairs. In the back of the house there is a square panelled room with a couch, telephone and stand. It overlooks a squat patch of grass. From that window I can see a warehouse. It is tall and hazel-brown and that is all there is to it. I do not stand in that window, except occasionally, to admire the grass. Once, I saw a child sitting out there, playing. It was pulling at the blades, grabbing handfuls and tugging, throwing the yellowing strands into the air. The child had a mean face and hair cropped so close to its head that I could view its sickly white scalp.

I had opened the window to caution the child against destroying what little grass there was. I slid open the pane and called, "Hey, be careful with that grass. There's not much left of it."

The child's head had lolled back, looking up at me with black eyes before loudly babbling words I could not decipher. It stared fiercely and I noticed its hands, the absence of thumbs. Grasping and quivering, it tore the grass. Babbling, it tossed handfuls up at me. The child was three or four but it knew not one word. It did not matter. What it had to say was realized on sight. It was the product of viciousness.

"Go home," I shouted, slamming the window and stepping back to my bedroom where I looked out to see the girl, naked and standing behind glass, arms placidly positioned by her sides, staring as if waiting for me. Pale and hurting. The faint remains of a bruise beneath her right eye. A swollen bottom lip invoking an image of inflamed innocence. All on the first day that I saw her.

Thinking back, I like to change things. I seem to believe that the girl and I have somehow been speaking. It is a feeling lodged in memory. Intimacy of one kind intends memories of another. But we know little of each other's pasts, removed from physical interaction, merely understanding the disburdening notion of compassion. Craving it. We are dim lovers like this. I have witnessed the violence of her secrets: her hurtful resignation, her defeated sense of complacency, each blow further strengthening our terms of mutual endearment.

The street is silent as I look down. Two big dogs trot into view, sloppily striding along the centre of the asphalt, sniffing the ground, sniffing each other, circling and trotting on. They are eager scroungers, like me with my carnal longings. I watch their rough paws strike the asphalt, catching like chafed skin against coarser flesh, the tangle of ruptured bodies splitting open to ingest each other.

I touch the curtains of my window. They are parted; I grip their edges and hold on. It is possible for me to dismiss all of this, pull my bedroom curtains closed, forget about these troubling thoughts of the girl and the abusive man I want so desperately to gouge from the picture. But he is a part of this now, perhaps a greater part than I first assumed, his presence further rousing our mournful desire for one another.

Releasing my left hand, I lower it and push against the place between my legs. This is how I choose to forget. My hand fits nicely against the hump and I let it rest there, sense myself growing with stiffening thoughts of the girl, penetrating and provocative notions that will fill her with merciful revelation. I will be her rescuer, delivering her from grief: simple pronouncements such as this.

Minutes beyond the unfolding of these thoughts, the girl appears, sits in her window, and stares instantly at me with a melancholic smile of hushed understanding. There are two long welts down the left side of her face and her top lip is swollen, making her appear younger than her years, provocatively unaware of what has become of her.

I slowly massage my groin. The erection pushes sleekly behind my trousers. I spread thumb and index finger and trace them against the thick outline. I am crying as I do this. I cry silently for her, and soon she joins me. Wiping at her face, she then runs a hand through her hair. Her shoulders shudder. When she raises her eyes, I see that her mouth is held weakly open. She is saying something, lips trembling as if pleading for forgiveness, then moving more fluently, perhaps reciting the lyrics of a slow song that might be our song. A radio beside her sighs sweetly— the verse astonishingly in sync with the fraudulent precepts of love she imagines will mend us, tempt us from our stations.

I undo my hasp, guide down the zipper. I smile invitingly for her. Leaving my trousers open, I inch down the front of my underwear, exposing the curved tip, the steadiness of the stiff veinwork. The air against my skin incites a pulse and my cock throbs as if wanting to split its own skin and gash itself down the centre, making me the vulnerable one.

The girl's lips continue stirring and she smiles with tears drenching her eyes. Her mouth holds a sentimental grimace as if recalling quieter times that have touched her. The blossoming of a thought seems uplifting, and she stands and walks off. In a short play of seconds, she returns with a double sheet of paper and re-takes her place. I watch her carefully guiding the marker in her right hand, adjusting and holding the paper across her knees. Done writing, she raises the sign and presses it to the window with both palms. I cannot make out the words, even though they are large and drawn in a black smear of ink. It is dark against the glass and only the inside is illuminated. The girl stands and steps back, now holding the paper with both hands in front of her face, and I plainly see the words. Three words in wide charcoal letters: CAN'T YOU SEE.

II

The mailman delivers bright and early. I wait for him on my step and he hands me the envelope, my unemployment cheque arriving as usual on its designated day. I will go to the bank and have it cashed. A resolution has been reached. Neglecting my financial obligations— the rent that must be paid in a matter of days— I decide to buy a present for the girl. Flowers. A classic portrait of kindness in the guise of fragrant petals. It will be a courtship. I will play the part for her. Help is something I must concern myself with.

At the corner of Field and Slattery, I turn with the Commerce Bank in sight. It is closed, but soon opens. A woman in a dark blue skirt and jacket stands behind the glass door turning a key. She is not smiling. Instead, she is thinking. Bolts snap open and a line of people from the neighbourhood silently enters. The staff know me here. They easily recognize the marred contours of my face. Without question, the teller stamps my cheque. No need for a second look. She snaps out the correct number of bills, then nods and stares past my shoulder to the next customer. I move across the shiny floor, pushing the fold of money into my deep loose pocket. Beyond the glass doors, the sunlight is brilliant in my eyes, its glare further assaulting me when I walk outside.

A bus screeches to a stop alongside me. The door folds open. I step up, lean forward, grip the rail and count three more steps. The bus driver regards me, then glances at the bill I drop into the glass receptacle. The bus driver is wearing large, silver shades that hold my warped reflection. He stares without comment. He tugs a long metal shaft and the doors fold shut. He checks his side mirror, and waits.

The bus will take me to the shopping mall. I will purchase flowers and gain entry to the girl's house. Once inside, I will feel her arms thrown around me, her wild kisses lavished upon each of my flawed features. I will accept her pledges of undying admiration. My tongue will fill her mouth and I will open her up, force myself inside until my pain is deeply buried— yet pushing— beneath the lacerated image she already holds of herself.

The flowers are shades of many colours: reds speckled black, purples with washes of yellow, whites tipped pink, wonderfully fragrant and wrapped in a blue paper cone.

I stand on the girl's doorstep. But first— before knocking— I glance back at my window, expecting to see myself standing there. It is my role to watch, and I feel strangely out of place positioned here, in the clarity of this picture. Snorting humourously at my sense of dislocation, I turn for the door, raise my hand, wet my lips, and knock. The sound resonates through the inner stairway, rising to her apartment door. I step back, my face burning with uncertainty.

"She there?" barks a voice from behind me. I pivot to see the man with the beard and skull-faced t-shirt, his hard eyes briskly surveying my flowers. I glance around but do not find his car. He is on foot today. A roaming pack of one.

The man smiles and his teeth are big, flat and dull. Tugging out his wallet, he pulls loose two fives. I see the back of his hand is tattooed, the outline of a blue heart with a blue arrow shot through it. He stuffs the bills into my hand and shoves away his wallet. When his hand comes around front, he snatches the flowers from me.

"BOOO," he shouts, stomping his black boot against the concrete stair.

I falter backward, watching as he fishes out a ring of keys and sorts through them with his thumb. There were no keys on his last visit, so I assume they belong to the girl. He has stolen them, made them his. Or perhaps they fit the doors to other rooms he visits, other women locked away, awaiting what he believes to be his bold and adventurous passion. I am almost at my door when he slips the key into the lock, turns the knob and moves in, kicking shut the barrier.

Turning my attention to the upper window, I see the girl standing there, close to the glass, looking down, gently shaking her head before it snaps back and she is dragged away. The man stands above her, spitting down. Kicking fast with his steel-toed boots.

An open-mouthed roaring rush for the drapes and they are tugged closed, the fabric stirring slightly, before their utter stillness provokes in me a lovelorn shiver of abandon.

The police are impotent in their bid to inhibit brutality. Their role is that of instructor, not enforcer. I have contacted them before concerning cries of women in the row houses to either side of me, but to no avail. Regardless, I call them now because this is all I am capable of. I explain to the switchboard operator. She indicates the proper department and puts me through. The policeman gives me his name. I outline the situation and he asks the address. He sighs while I am speaking, then explains that they have been there twice since the girl took up residence after complaints from neighbours in the houses that adjoin hers. Many complaints against this woman. The policeman tells me where she has lived before. Each address. He runs through her file, flatly reading the street names and numbers and frequency of police visits. "We send a car every time," he says. "She won't press charges. Scared. And then beaten again. In with the wrong crowd. They'd kill her if she pressed charges. All of them've been locked away. Couldn't care less. Happens over and over. One day a punch connecting with the odds. Snap. A fall. Dead. She's bagged up and they're off smacking another woman around."

The policeman apologizes for his lack of influence. "I'm sorry," he says. "You need for someone to kill that kind of scum. Just kill them. What jury would convict a man who did that? Who would?"

I tell the policeman I do not know.

"My hands are tied," he insists. He keeps me on the line, explaining what they try to do, how they attempt to persuade women away from such situations. The programs that are offered. The shelters. "Futility," he says. He says, "Jesus, I've seen them half blind. Purple faces swollen so they can only nod yes or no. Cut open and denying it even though the blood's running out of them. Denying who did it with the guy standing right next to them, blood on his knuckles." The policeman says, "I'm sorry. Believe me. Nothing happens. But, I tell you what, we'll send a car anyway. For your sake."

I thank the policeman and set the receiver down, step from the small room in the back of the house, up the hallway, toward my bedroom. I step close to a view of what I am expecting. The drapes are open across the street and the girl is standing in her window, naked with blood clotted beneath her nostrils and upper lip, smeared along her chin.

There are bruises on her chest, others speckled down her left shin. The man is nowhere in sight. He has moved on to other revitalizing havens.

Leaning against the glass, the girl stumbles slightly to the side, limps and skips awkwardly to maintain balance. She holds up the same crumpled shivering sign: CAN'T YOU SEE.

I take my time undressing for her. Slowly, I unbutton my shirt and draw it away from my arms, step out of my trousers and underwear: one foot, then the other. I show her what it should be like. How it is meant to be.

Standing naked in my window, I delicately trace the air as if it holds the outline of her body. I kiss the pale underbelly of my own arm, lovingly peck each rounded fingertip. I caress my hard breasts, my waist, my thighs. All the while, I watch her. I see the sign drift from her hands, settling on the floor where she steps on it with both bare feet. The paper sticks to her skin. It is a touching sight, her futile attempt to kick it free. But soon her will is crippled and she begins to sob, thudding her forehead against the glass, progressively harder and with conviction, as if its rupture will make us well.

St. John's, 1989

Above the Movements of Night

for Katie

Crouched low in the woods, beneath the wide splay of spruce branches, Thomas Neary secures a snare along the trail of the rabbit's run. Carefully he twirls the wire's end around a notched root and slowly opens the hoop to a width slightly smaller than his fist. Done with setting the wire four fingers from the ground, he stands and glances behind his boot heels— green and rust-coloured bog, brittle brush, and young low trees— before stepping back and waiting.

Several robins shrill high in the evergreens. He is amazed at how big the red breasts are out this way, as one flashes through the high branches and bursts off with a shiver of brown wings, darting skyward.

Thomas Neary stares down at the place where he has set his snare, the hoop of thin picture wire that will stop the rabbit in its tracks; quickly, he hopes, always feeling somehow discomfitted by what he is doing here, by the fate that his life has aligned him with, a man abiding in an untrue skin, and lingering now, not moving on, waiting to see what might happen beyond this wrongful sense of conviction.

The woods smell of morning. He recalls the sound of bacon and eggs frying in the camp he left behind just after sunrise, the smell of it in the air, the taste of its fat still in his mouth. He remembers, believing the meal filled him this morning, but is vaguely uncertain. He swats at the air in front of his face. A tiny black fly. Perhaps his memory is from the day before.

A flicker low to the ground, the small brush startled by movement, tiny leaves rustle as grey fur moves closer along the above-ground tunnel of rabbit run, then makes it to the wire, partially through the hoop and stops. A dangerous, breathtaking trick.

After several minutes, Thomas Neary bends down to loosen the wire, his slow exhale in the hollows of his ears, his fingers working nimbly as they raise the soft warmness of fur and hold it in his hands, studying the perfect shape of it, the legs and the ears, the plump body, before turning slightly at his waist and lifting the flap of his satchel, dropping the rabbit in. The look of it curled there, lying against the faded innards of the leather pouch. The flap closing over to trap one tiny muddled heartbeat.

His daughter, Robin, is still sleeping in her bunk at the camp when he arrives. Pitch, as Robin named the black Labrador Retriever, has been watching over the child but now comes out, walking lazily, its big body tired in the sun that is beginning to burn its brightest as the day moves closer to noon. It pauses beside Thomas and looks up, glances at the satchel, then leads its master into the cabin where it stands by the side of Robin's bed, staring up at Thomas, who stares down at the girl.

"Robin?" Thomas whispers, lifting the strap of his satchel over his head and laying it on the wobbly table beside him, then— displeased with its position— lifting the strap again to hook it on a rusty spike head protruding from the log wall.

The child does not stir and Pitch whines once and drops down with its belly on the floor, its head on its front paws, its yellow eyes fearfully watching under the bed.

"Robin?" Thomas whispers. "Sweetheart?" The child moves softly against the old mattress, her plump face turning toward Thomas as she rolls over and, with eyes still shut, tilts her head up against the grey pillow, her tiny bottom lip pushing out, her skin so pale with only a hint of pink, her hair curly and long, so that Thomas has to smile and bend to her, kiss her on the top of her warm head and whisper funny things in her ear, phrases he has told her since she was a baby, speaking this way until she is lured from slumber into the gentle confidence of his ways. Eyes remaining closed, a secret smile slowly brightens her face.

The rain makes the tree trunks darker and wet. The evergreen boughs sway lightly and the leaves of the dense dogberry and maple trees sag under the continuous downpour, everything so very green and alive in the light, faithfully drawing in moisture.

Thomas and Robin watch through the window, the rain coming straight down, not touching the small pane of glass.

Robin sits in her t-shirt and underwear and stares into the wet woods, then regards her father, the side of his face where he is watching the outdoors.

"Are you cold?" he asks, not looking at her, but then turning to see her eyes, smiling quietly.

Robin shakes her head. "Where's Pitch gone?"

Thomas Neary shrugs and stares at the rain again. "Out, I guess."

"He must be getting really wet."

"He's okay, he always liked the rain."

"I think we should go out and look for him."

"No." A bank of lightning flashes low in the sky on the distant horizon. In the daylight its power is not so brilliant. "Lightning," Thomas says. "Did you see that?" He catches Robin staring at his face.

She shakes her head. "I think we should go look for Pitch."

"He'll be fine."

Robin joins her hands and lets them rest on the table. Then she leans against the edge, pressing it into her stomach.

"How long more for this rain?" she asks.

"I'll turn it off for you," he says and peeks at her, smiling, to see that she is smiling, too.

"You can't turn it off," she laughs, her voice ringing out in the small cabin.

"Oh, yes," he says, "I can do anything. I'm your dad. Remember?"

The light from the lamp hisses quietly, giving off a delicate glow that leaves the shadows dark toward the corners. Thomas Neary plays solitaire and Robin watches from her chair at the table. He can feel the heat from the lamp against his face and so he reaches for the small steel wheel to adjust the glow, turning it down slightly so that the flame recedes within the delicate mesh bag that hisses and glows like special fire when turned up very high, but low now, yellow and orange at once.

The rain stopped moments before and there is that distinct silence that is realized only after the quiet has lingered for a play of moments. From outside, a howling resonates far off, a rough painless howling that has been there for most of the night, but smothered by the rain. Now, the sound is clearer, easily recognizable, fully itself.

"There he is," Robin says, getting out of her chair and going to the door.

"Don't open it," her father warns, his voice stern, knowing the practicality of keeping things shut at night. "The bugs," he says, "coming for the light. They'll eat us."

Robin steps back from the door and goes to her father's side, pressing closer against his arm, holding it and staring down at the cards that he lays out, not knowing what they mean, what the faces and designs are supposed to signify.

"How do you play that?" she asks, touching one of the cards with a small finger.

Thomas Neary looks at her, accustomed to her questions, seeing only pleasure in her face, thinking— as always— *You'll learn*, but saying instead, "I'll teach you, one day. I'll try and teach you. But you're too young, now. It wouldn't make any sense if I tried."

"Bed time," she says and nods at him, wrongfully interpreting his tone as a portent of dismissal.

Pitch is there in the morning, sitting in the wild grass at the front of the camp. Robin runs to the dog and drops to her knees, hugging its warm black fur, then scratching its ears. The sun is up and the air is filled with what the heat does to the dampness of fallen rain that now lingers in the growth around them.

"He's here," Robin calls back toward the open doorway.

Thomas Neary stands there and watches. Smiling, he glances off toward the woods and remembers that they forgot to eat last night. The child did not mention a word about hunger. Food did not come to mind. Nor do they seem to be in want of breakfast.

"How wonderful," Thomas tells himself, leaving the doorway and moving out into the crisp morning. He steps toward his daughter and bends to pick her up, groaning playfully as he rises. "You're getting heavy."

Robin laughs wildly, and Thomas spins in circles with her weight in his arms trying to pull him off balance, but confident with his feet against the firm ground, stepping choppily, confined, then stopping, but everything still spinning, the trees and the land and sky needing to slow to catch up with them.

With startled awe, Robin falls silent, watching the sky, then her father's face, as Thomas moves toward the woods to show his daughter the varied shapes and veins of the leaves, the hidden animal trails that must be made familiar, the magical sifting of sunlight through the limbs that he knows will fill her with the wonder he wishes her never to lose.

In the patch of wild grass behind them, Pitch sits there watching as the man carries the child toward the forest. It sneezes once, then scratches its face with its paw, its mouth stretched in a way that implies profound amusement. Rising fully on its legs and following, its tongue hangs out as it hurries its pace, panting toward the shrill laughter that echoes out from the trees.

"Daaaadddy!" a child's voice, like brilliance reflecting in the wet forest, shimmering here and there. A series of shrieks as nature's provocation, the bright sound piercing through walls of the solitary cabin, deeper still, through the dark, forgotten confines of Thomas' leather satchel; the stirrings of a warming rabbit, two ears twitching, heartbeat remembering, dauntlessly thrilled to life.

St. John's, 1993

A Coward

I am instructed to sit in a high-backed wooden chair. Across from me, a small woman with a bony elongated face will not look up; her fingers are tensely spread across the ebony table-top. She is naked, her whitish skin hanging loose, as if gradually unbinding from her shrinking frame. Her hair is clipped short, a curly tangle of coarse black weeds.

I cannot stop myself from staring at her wrinkled breasts and belly, her purplish-black nipples, her racks of ribs and her fingers that reach between her legs to scoop out a palm full of sand. Raising her arm to the table-top, she tilts her hand, allowing the sand to slip into a neat pile.

Three times since my arrival earlier today the woman has begun to hum with a clumsiness that alters the composition of her face, the bony features shifting like knuckles smoothly displacing and setting themselves beneath skin.

Naturally, the clock on the wall has stopped. Sing has seen to that. After sitting me in this chair, and before leaving, he violently struck the clock's face with the tarnished brass head of his cane. The head is shaped like a fat lady's, her mouth jammed open, bolstering one long feverish note.

The smashing of the face and then the laughter as the glass face of the clock shattered and jingled a tune onto the floor. Sing's musical fingers reached in and bent the hands of the clock until they were pointing at me, arrowheads waiting to lurch toward their target.

. Pulling back his hand, a turncoat piece of glass tilted loose, slicing into Sing's skin, lodging more deeply as he drew away. He gave the wound little notice, but simply plucked out the shard of glass and let it drop without word or exclamation.

Small splotches of his blood have dried against the white floor, the stains in the obtuse pattern of wings, an inner charge finally freeing itself, anticipating ascent. I grin at the maudlin humour of it.

Sing said, "Sit and face this image of disgrace." I translate as best I can. His actual words did not rhyme so sickly. He was speaking in his own tongue, music: the synthetic representation of smooth and abrupt movements, a language whose exact translation continues to defy me.

"You're a coward," the woman says without looking up, her right hand lifting the sand that drains from her cunt. I stare down at the fingers of her left hand. She is concentrating on moving them— mere centimetres at a time— back and forth across the table-top. She desires to touch me, but her nerve is weak.

"You keep coming apart," she insists, nodding slightly. "One leg, one arm, one eye." Swallowing with difficulty, her eyes remain dipped down, flitting about. She lifts her hand from the table and slowly presses two fingertips along her chest, counting her lean ribs with a contradictory look of humility and displeasure. "What you've done," she whispers, flatly.

I stand and step away from the table, stare down at my legs. I bend them at the knees, lifting one foot, then lowering it. Doing the same with the other— slowly up, slowly down. I blink and widen my eyes to prove a point, to take inventory. I hold up my arms, turn my palms over, exposing the furrowed lifelines.

"Two of everything," I tell her.

"That's not what I meant," she counters defensively, "not at all." Her eyes darken but she is still unable to steal a glance at me. "Why don't you focus some attention away from yourself for once? Give me a rest."

Some time later, the lights are switched off. The room vanishes around us, and the woman begins to hum dreadfully. The humming grows nearer until it appears to be above me. I tilt back my head and stare at the uniformly black ceiling. The humming listlessly descends. Soon, it lingers close to my ear. I sense the woman's cool gentle breath lapping and thrilling my skin. Her fingers sneaking through my hair. It is her hand crawling there; a parasite, as exact as me, ingesting resolution and vomiting doubt.

My pores open up for her. They gape for entry. Lips press to mine, then lift away. Thicker, protruding flesh is set against my lips, my teeth.

"A coward's consolation," her squeaky voice assures me. "But it's a rare recovery." I open my mouth to taste her chafed nipple. It is cracked and

blood-black from years of suckling. Her breasts are hollow and the skin hangs
helplessly. I lick the nipple and roll it between my thumb and index finger until
it is hard, then softer, ripe. I clutch her with both hands around her bony back
and lunge her toward me, suck the purplish-black fluid from her nipple. It is
bitter and murky. An unexpected sob catches in my breath as I reach down for
the place between her legs and feel her baldness, her sagging soft lips. I slip my
fingers in. But something nips savagely at my fingertips and I draw back.

"Just finish something," she says, gripping the back of my head with both
her callous hands, forcing my mouth against her collapsed breast, her ribs digging
into the side of my face. "Finish this. Every drop, you selfish little boy."

I think myself toward the year and time and am quickly snatched up in
the resonance, sped along.

My memory goes like this:

There is a car crash on a dark stretch of highway. A Renault Le Car
has struck a moose, veered off and raced up a bank on a slant, only to
tumble onto its side, back onto the asphalt.

The moose lies at the edge of the highway, close to the ridge of a
depthless chasm. The headlights of the car lend the moose an ominous
appearance. The animal struggles to stand on its thin spindly legs, but
they buckle. Thrusting its dense bulk to the side, it stumbles and drags
itself nearer to the edge. Straining to escape the splintered bones that
serve no purpose, it finds the ledge and soundlessly drops over.

I hear the low disoriented moan of a woman. Stepping for the car,
I see her in the driver's seat, her leg torn loose above the knee, ruptured
by the steering column and slashed by a webbed sheet of windshield
glass. The bottom half of her leg hangs by a flimsy wedge of skin. The
crash victim's arm has been crushed by the buckled form of the
dashboard forced upon her. The mechanical lever of the directional
signal has struck the woman's slumped head just above the cheek,
propelling her left eye from its socket. The eyeball revolves toward
me, dangling in a way that tempts refitting.

The radio is playing in the otherwise absolute silence that follows the busted tangle of metal and glass. Its signal is spastic, like the revolution of a warped record. It is from this oblong sound that Sing takes shape. He has been injured as well. This explains the cane. Full verses of songs have been shattered by the impact, agility rammed and dented, the chorus missing teeth and, subsequently, the rhyme has lost its meter.

The woman is moaning painfully, perhaps beginning to plead for help, but I will not step any nearer. I watch the blood drain against her white blouse. She is not wearing a brassiere and her shivering breasts are wetly hugged by the flowing red material. Flinching, her flesh jars in an intriguing manner, her nipples erect as her blood drips onto the pavement.

The horror of the scene has charged it with a dream-like intensity that is consumptive. Intriguingly personal. I sense the erection, but am too cowardly to climb on top of this dying woman and feed the life back into her. To brush my cock against the blood of her severed leg, to dampen myself and slip easily inside her, to challenge what flows so cordially from her opened, needy body.

I wish my lips wet with the agony of her wounds, my tongue in her mouth, chasing the darting pain, my fingertips pressing into her soaked breasts, my red palm prints everywhere, touching her, dreaming of coming apart like her, so conveniently, with no apology, ever, to anyone.

Sing stands by the vehicle, bent slightly and staring in. I hear the vague speculative tinkling of his breath. The dome light fills this inner darkness. The dim headlights reach weakly forward. Surroundings are washed black by night. Sing cannot touch this woman. She is suffering with such extremity that her hearing is jammed.

Sing attempts a recitation, a calming verse, a romantic number from the '30s, but the words are tattered. He glances over at me, then nods severely toward the woman, insisting that I help her. But I will not move. I fear her pain. I fear her pain will touch me, become mine, bullying its way through my fingertips, plotting the memory stronger, closer, more explicit through the cordiality of touch.

This sense of trepidation startles other incidents of cowardice to life. They take shape from the reek of gasoline, in the ambivalent shadows surrounding the crashed car: I see myself in a field as a child. My friends have released a hamster from its cage. They take turns shooting at the rodent with pellet rifles. It is struck and topples over, struggles to run lopsided. Another hit. I watch, wait for death to claim the convulsing hamster and then— once we have cleared off, gone home— I secretly return later to bury the hamster in a corner of the field, and say a prayer. I bow down to God, even in the faithless noise of my anger.

My time in the army. Cowardly subservience meaning to strengthen us as soldiers. Commands to be followed without question. All of this as a means of fortifying character, of instilling bravery. One single charge of men acting together in force. These flagrant acts of singlemindedness the worst possible gusts of cowardice. We were stationed in Cyprus where we visited the whores shipped in from the Philippines. I would not touch them for fear of sexual ineptness. But I had to play along. I could not have the other men thinking that I was of another sexual persuasion. I could not endure them taunting me.

There was one woman I joined in the whorehouse hotel room. I paid her to sit still, to be silent. I merely wanted to watch her, to find comfort and appreciation in her love-lost face.

"I just want to look at you," I instructed in simple English. I stood a few feet away from her and— as the minutes passed— witnessed her features soften from whore to nervous darling and then to whore again, becoming angered by the thought that I was somehow insulting her. Not touching at all, she believed I must be some type of inhuman freak for not taking from her what I had paid for.

Years later in the mountains of Spain, I settled in the white village of Mijas, where I offered circular donkey rides for twenty-five pesetas, near the shrine of Nortre Dame La Virgin de la Pena. Our Lady, The Virgin of the Rock.

My skin grew dark like a Spaniard's and I came to speak the language. Tourists arrived, spent their allotted money at the cafes and stalls peddling castanets with painted scenes, leather purses of all sorts, postcards of villages and religious monuments, and brittle terra cotta pottery. Once having acquired their looted piece of another land, the tourists departed.

I knew no one there, and so I stayed. The Spanish residents did not bother me. If they asked questions, I simply replied, "Yo no se." I do not know. And— truthfully— I did not want to know.

I rented a room in a modest white house and, at night, watched the distant valleys far below. The clusters of small white villages flickered warmly with light. Bats swirled and fluttered among the large-leafed trees and the language softly rose to me like calm signals, affirming my unconditional detachment.

When the natives celebrated and danced during their fiestas, I watched with a cold heart, an outsider who could never partake. For six years I lived this life, alone.

Like all true cowards I was a foreigner in a strange land, adrift in a void without fear of connection or commitment or chance meetings with acquaintances hungry for news of recent material acquisitions and social accomplishments.

I acquired nothing and accomplished even less.

My only preoccupation was visitations to the shrine— Nortre Dame La Virgin de la Pena. It was a small cave in a grassy hill that rested precariously along the ledge of a misty gorge. Outside, there was a marble tile promenade with a modest metal fountain and a white statue marking the site. Inside, the light was very faint, the space no more than fifteen feet in width and length. Grey wrought-iron benches were set in rows before the altar where clustered candles were lit. To one side, a slight alcove displayed a blue and gold statue of the Virgin Mary. A low-wattage red light shone up from a place beneath the statue, out of sight, richly illuminating the rough clay walls of the cave. And pinned to walls was an intimate assortment of items. Small school photographs of children, pictures of men and women of all ages, healthy and smiling, or sick in bed. Maybe dead, each of them. There were strips of clothing stuck to the soft rock, pieces of velvety ribbons, and whole braids of children's silky hair, snipped off and hung as offerings to make the giver well.

The sight of all of this disturbed me to no end, but I faithfully returned. I felt strangely at home among such disarming grief.

Then, without warning, as these things are prone to occur, there was a connection. The death of my mother drew me back to North America, to sights I recalled with the bland expansiveness of childhood boredom relived.

By the time I received word from the army— who knew of my whereabouts in order to forward my pension cheque— my mother had already been buried beside my father, having left instructions with the funeral parlour. I had missed the ceremony. I was left only to deal with her house. How could I dismantle her home? I decided that I must keep it. The memories were rich and plentiful. A coward can never kill his memories, no matter how much they displease or provoke him.

For most of my adult life, I had understood that following the death of my mother, there would be no need for me to work. She had been a wealthy woman. Adequate money would be willed to provide for me. I was certain of this.

Neighbours telephoned to offer condolences but— following the first few pitifully awkward encounters— I would neither answer the telephone nor the door.

A few days later, I discovered from my mother's attorney that a deed was left for land and a cabin in an area I knew nothing of. The attorney called me to his office and quietly— with dignity and reserve— presented me with the deed and a note which read:

I hope you're well. I speak to you now from another place. It's a strange thing that you can still hear my voice with these words. But never mind. I'm sure such thoughts would be of no interest to you. I've chosen a place for you myself. Deep in the woods where I know you'll be at peace.

I must say that I've regretted your distance for all the years you avoided me and your father. From your early years I understood you'd be alone. The magnets that draw us to other people are misdirected in you. Your fear (or is it selfishness?) has reversed the magnets so that you are drawn only inside, toward yourself. Your father died an unhappy death. He called out for you. His final word— your name, over and over again. He wanted you by his side, but you ignored his needs. He could never understand your discharge from the army. He hoped a higher rank of you, but your progress was nil and riddled— as always— with irksome apathy. Your occasional cards from foreign countries only reaffirmed your inability to truly love. The drifter fears love. Those who will not care for or assist others are lacking the love of God, of spirit, of depth. I hope you enjoy your place in the wilderness.

I've instructed my attorney to sell the house and auction off all the possessions. The money will be donated to a charity of your choice.

I am truly sorry for what I have to say to you, but I am dying now and your absence is making me so very alone. I hope we can find each other on more loving terms in the next life.

I'm still your mother and I hope to see you in the hereafter.

The note was signed: *I love you always, even from my grave, Mom.*

I know that she expects me to visit her grave site, but I will not. What is the purpose of graveyards? Why are people so set on visiting a site where only bones are buried, when the spirit loiters in your thoughts constantly?

Two weeks later I am on the highway. Engine trouble necessitates a four-hour stop-over in a small town named Cutland Junction, where the mechanics are friendly but speak in a way I can barely understand.

It is dusk before I resume my journey. The road map indicates that I am a little less than one hour from the cottage that my mother has left for me. The sky darkens as I drive toward it: ominous blue brooding toward a haunting violet that threatens to meld into a consoling black.

My headlights gradually brighten, become solid, reaching off-shoots. They illuminate the darkness in their path but leave the night air unchanged once past.

Up ahead, in startling disunity, I see two lights— one on top of the other. Only as I cautiously glide nearer do I realize that the lights belong to a car set on its side. The image is unnerving, as are all uncommon sights on a seemingly endless, deserted stretch of black highway.

I pull over, quietly shut off my lights and lean out onto the still, hard asphalt. Stepping toward the crashed car, I hear the moose as it drags itself to the chasm and hurls itself over.

Then I detect the low stunned moaning of a woman. The radio crackles and dies, comes back to life, the car's headlights reaching forward like ghost arms, pulsing.

The dome light within dims and brightens, like a dissonant strobe on a dance floor, revealing the woman's white complexion and the red that is splashed across her face like obscene make-up. Her one eye painfully opens and closes, wanting to be its own separate living thing, to break clear in a way that would ensure its own survival.

I listen to the music, trying to piece the song together. I never was an admirer of music. It is noise, disunity. But from the music, my limping persecutor takes shape. The expression on Sing's face indicates his disagreeable mission. He cannot help the woman, so he will hum the tune of empathy, hopeful that I might hum along.

Suffering my indifference, he grudgingly relents and simply stares at the crippled female. Her low moaning fades out and the headlights brighten for an instant before dimming to an understandable low.

"She's gone," says Sing, turning and leaning on his cane. Without further word, he takes hold of my arm— as if for support— and leads me back to my car. His grip is friendly, or so I assume. "I know the way," he ventures as I spark the ignition. "Your mother was a great lover of music. The cottage she built for you is only minutes away."

At his direction, I take the appropriate turn off the highway, rolling onto a gravel pot-holed road. A rust-coloured fox scoots in front of the car, but freezes instantly, its thin body turned to face us. It stares into the headlights.

I slow the vehicle by simply touching the brake.

Sing hums and the fox flinches and scurries away. I begin to understand. I see it in Sing's doughy, complacent face— the ease with which his inflections direct this world. By simply tapping his cane like a baton, he sustains the desired intensity of pitch, sets the melodious framing, the categorizing of memory to time.

And how we love to remember when the tune plays!

"It's just up here a little ways," Sing says, tapping the window with the head of his cane, indicating a gap between two towering spruce. Rolling slowly nearer, I see by the headlights that two wide tree trunks frame a gravel drive. I pull in between them and carefully journey down toward the summer cottage at the end of the road.

The cottage is small and— in the discerning sense of the word— beige. White light spills from the windows, mutely illuminating the low tangle of burgundy bushes and the grassy overgrown fronting. I step from the car to find Sing already by my side. He leads me through the door, into the single room where he sits me at the ebony table.

"Enough of this estrangement," he says, tapping his cane and then sweeping it in the direction of my limbs. "Time to face the music."

I gaze across the table, see the naked woman with the bony elongated face, the bland bumps shifting beneath her skin. Without uttering another word, Sing smashes the face of the clock and points the arrowheaded hands straight at me.

There are no mysteries. Memory inevitably decodes everything.

The fleeting instants of so-called "present" find dimension in recall. Who would be so asinine as to believe there exists anything as preposterous as "the future"? Only in memory can one know the present, only in the past— after it has presented itself. Never while occurring.

When I touch an object, I feel it as a past sensation. When I think, I am aware only after the idea has been realized. When I speak, I hear the words in memory. An object must move before I recognize its movement.

The bony-faced woman with the empty, hollow breasts is so scarred and ugly now. I remember her when, as a child, I behaved in accordance with her conscientious directives. She thrilled me like no one else. A clean slate.

But then my thoughts turned stormy, reckless with adolescent uncertainty, and she grew old before her time. Lies and guilt savaged her.

She sits there now, afraid to lift her fingers from the table, petrified to touch me. She hums in the dim room, in the uncertain light, and waits with a weary look of longing for me to end it between us, once and for all. She is willing now. She has had enough.

Mustering the courage to peek up at me, to meet my eyes, to face me as the pathetic wretch that I am, "Don't be such a gutless wonder," she spitefully insists. "Murder me."

St. John's, 1989

Muscle

True things.

That's what he thought as he held the man down in the dark parking lot:

1. The only way a person can be deeply changed (swayed from what's bred in the bone) is through trauma.

The man tried to stir and Juke Ash tightened his grip, holding a shoulder in each fist and pressing down with his knee into the man's ribs. He watched the changing look on the face beneath him. There was something starting there that might sway his mind one way or the other, and so he quickly shifted to brace a forearm against the man's throat.

A car came up behind them, its headlights brightening the fearful expression on the man's face, its tires dully popping over gravel before it stopped.

Juke Ash looked plainly over his shoulder as the headlights were switched off and he saw the orange parking lights and the shadow of the thin woman who stepped out from behind the wheel turning sideways to glance around.

2. The face must be exceptional in order to excuse small breasts in a woman.

"Larry?" the woman called, facing Juke, "Is that you?" She shaded her eyes and squinted as if the darkness was too much for her. She was wearing a black dress with a single string of white pearls and black mesh nylons that gave her legs a slender shape.

"Stay down," Juke barked at the man.

"Larry?"

"Go away," Juke Ash said quietly, staring into the man's frightened eyes, but talking to the woman.

"No." She came closer, stepping off to the side to have a better view.

"Let Larry up," she said crossly when Juke glanced at her. He saw that she was the woman he remembered, only appearing slightly different with her face made up and her hair done.

3. The difference between a relationship and a marriage is that in a relationship you discuss and share ideas; in a marriage you argue about them.

Another car pulled out of its parking space and rolled up alongside them, this one to the left of Juke. With the headlights on his face like a threat, he leaned harder, his forearm pressing firmly into the man's windpipe so there was a spitting, croaking sound. Juke noticed the shade of the man's lips, the headlights making the purple swollen texture very plain.

"He can't breathe," the woman called out, alarmed. One step forward, a stomp of her high-heeled shoe against the gravel; she almost slipped.

Headlights from the second car dimmed to park and instants later two doors slammed, almost in unison.

4. It is possible to rationalize any act, as long as it is your act and not another's.

The woman knelt with one hand flat to the gravel. Juke could hear her breathing as she leaned closer, could smell the sweet flowery scent of her perfume.

"That's not Larry," she said.

Juke heard her stand and felt her hand slapping him heavily on the back. "That's not him," she snapped, blowing out air and cursing.

"Oh." Juke released the pressure from his forearm and stood, swiping dirt from the knees of his jeans, then straightening the sleeves of his black shirt where they were rolled up to his elbows.

The man weakly touched his throat as Juke gazed down at him.

5. In order to create a monster, you have to make it human first.

One of the two men sitting against the hood of the car laughed quietly. The other one kicked at the gravel to see the dust rise.

"He's still inside," the woman said. "Larry's like him, but taller." She turned and moved back toward her car. Juke heard a soft dinging sound when she opened the door. "Get it right this time," she called, then glanced at the two men.

Juke Ash spun without a word and stomped toward the bar. Once inside, he chose a face like the other, but with a taller body, and walked toward it, ignoring the people who cared to watch.

6. A woman will always forgive you, as long as she loves you and you know how to make her laugh.

True things, Juke told himself as he grabbed the new man and dragged him out into the parking lot. He held onto the man's shirt and hit him quickly, again and again, until he was limp and hanging from Juke's shivering grip.

Juke took a deep breath and let the body drop, his foot against the new man's face.

"Don't," the man mumbled.

"That's him," the woman said, coming up from behind. Juke

turned and looked at her face and saw sourness there. Taking off one of her high-heeled shoes, she dropped down on her knees and began beating the man in the head, holding the shoe with both hands and lashing down.

7. *How true things get out is through the body.*

The two men sitting against the hood of their car clapped loosely as Juke swung back his leg and kicked the man. One of them said, "You got it right this time, Jukey."

Burnt Head, 1994

A Natural Thing

Teresa sits in the claw-foot bathtub slipping a bar of soap across her left shoulder, then down between her buoyant breasts. Light from the overhead low-wattage bulb brushes her skin with an enticing sheen— her body appearing softer than usual— and she is noticeably pleased as she surveys her chest.

I watch with something more than interest. The mood is obvious. It is a touching display, her exhibitionism delighting her as well. Guiding her hands through the water, Teresa marvels at the fresh, captivating sound. She peeks at me and smiles with her lips closed, then shuts her eyes tightly, sliding her body down. The flat shimmying noise of her backside moving against the porcelain incites memories of childhood.

Staying under for a while, she does not move, baiting me. Then she resurfaces with a rush of noise, and one long deep breath, as she wipes at her face then peers at me with the same secret smile.

"Christie?" she calls, sinking low in the tub while continuing to watch me above the white tarnished rim, the look in her eyes implying that a treat is forthcoming. Drawing her attention away from my face, she turns her head to watch the mahogany bathroom door, and calls again, a touch louder.

The door is half open. I can see sunlight spilling in from the front windows. It is yellowish-white and slants across the edge of the rug, barely touching the hardwood floor that runs throughout the entire second-floor apartment. The living space is nicely decorated. Particularly attractive is the bathroom, its walls painted peach with thick off-white mouldings and intricately hand-carved baseboards. To my left, the sink is deep and fitted with brass faucet and taps. The hardwood floor is a darker, richer brown in here, and there are several thick rugs in place, one before the toilet, another by the door, one next to the tub. Teresa prides herself on her love of all things old and quaint. She spends most of the large sums of money she receives from her ex-husband on such purchases, finding comfort in these accommodating, well-worn articles of the past.

I am here by early-morning invitation. Teresa on the telephone: "I'm taking a bath," she teased. "You know what I look like wet. How it feels. That smell you love." A mild giggle, before she whispered: "I'll let you dry all the wet spots."

I hear the words again as I lean back and place both palms flat against the wall behind me. Lifting a leg, I bend it at the knee and set my toes against the edge of the baseboard. Without a word, I watch Teresa as she smiles neatly at me and cleanses her skin with even, form-shaping strokes.

"Smile," she says, chewing on the corner of the blue facecloth, sucking and chewing. When she sees that I will not smile, she gives up. "I love the taste of this." She splashes the cloth down into the water and scowls at me. "Come on! What's the matter with you?... Smile for once."

"If you say so." But I do not smile. Instead, I move my tongue around in my mouth, slip it along the backs of my bottom teeth, wonder when Teresa's daughter will appear, the child she has been calling for.

"I say so." Her eyes punish me, but then she flippantly blows me a kiss. "Come on, sweetie." Her hands float under water, above her pink thighs. She stares down, letting her fingers sway against the pull of underwater pressure.

Without the sound of footsteps, her daughter appears in the bathroom doorway, wearing a white cotton nightdress with a wide lace collar and loose pink socks on her feet. A thick crop of blonde curls hangs straight down her back. I glance at her face. The dimple in her chin sweetens her appearance. A small pug nose works equally well to charm me. Stepping in, her feet are small and soundless, her eyes sleepy, filled with quiet complacency.

Staring at me for a moment, she then says, "Yes?" but she is answering her mother's call. Her eyes will not leave me. They are curious. Yawning, she languidly raises one cupped hand to her mouth.

"This is Kevin," says Teresa. "The one I've been telling you about. Remember?"

Christie nods.

"Say hi, baby."

"Hi," she says. Moving close to the toilet, she lifts the lid, inches up her nightdress and casually sits. A moment later water trickles into the toilet, spurting, then streaming out. Christie offers a weak smile, holding the edge of her nightdress high above her waist. Her stomach is slightly plump and her belly button turned inward, concealed. Still watching me, she lifts and bends one leg, pulling off a sock, then letting it fall to the floor. She does the same with her other leg, then she stands and wipes herself with a small fold of tissue before the fabric of her nightdress drops down around her ankles. She does not flush the toilet. Instead, she backs away until the position of the bathtub stops her from reversing further. She reaches behind, sliding her hands along the porcelain rim and lifting herself slightly, going up on her toes, all the while regarding me.

Stepping toward the toilet, I watch how she stretches until she cannot hold herself any longer and laughs, dropping to the flats of her feet. I give her a confident smile, reach for the toilet lever and push it down. "Okay?" I say above the rushing sound of water inside the tank. Christie's eyes fill with spectacular amusement. She yawns again with a generous smile on her lips.

"I was going to do that," she says, almost laughing. "After you finish. Your turn now."

"My turn?" I say, my eyes questioning Teresa, wondering about the play of Christie's words. But Teresa merely growls. The sound is husky.

"Go ahead," she insists, watching her hands drift closer to the water's surface. "It's educational." She tilts back her head, lifting her nose higher to adopt a grim, proper expression. "Curiosity. You know, old chap, and all that. Give it a go."

"I'll do it," says Christie, quickly stepping forward. Using both anxious hands, she struggles to unclip the hasp of my trousers. Her blonde brow wrinkles in concentration until the hasp pops loose. Then she is happy. She could not be happier than at that moment. I see it in her face as she glances up to meet my eyes. Easily guiding the zipper, she reaches in with both sets of fingers and takes hold of me.

"I like to aim it," she says, confidently staring at my face. "Turn the other way." Her shoulders go limp and she tilts her head in a chastising manner, her body squirming a little. "You have to turn, silly. That way." Nodding at the toilet, she tries to move me, coaxing my hip with her insistent elbow. I take my time turning, allowing her short legs to shuffle along with me.

"Go on," she says. "Do it." My stomach muscles tighten and I force down on my bladder. It takes a long while for even a few drops to escape. Then a quick blast of urine shoots into the toilet, followed by another. Soon a smooth unbroken stream flows out of me.

"It's funny," she says, smiling back at her mother. She playfully aims my penis, shooting for the inner rim of the bowl, then for the water, back and forth, listening to the differing sounds. She does not look at me when she says hesitantly, as if she knows she's giving something away, "Mommy has one in the drawer."

"My secrets," Teresa gasps dramatically, lifting the back of her arm to her forehead. "Honey child, don't tell all my secrets."

The child stares at me as she pulls her nightdress over her head. Her blonde hair falls loose when the material drops to the floor. Clumsily lifting one foot into the tub, she rests a moment, sitting on the rim with one leg in and one leg out. A shiver rises gooseflesh across her body. "It's cold," she says, staring down. She slouches forward, holding the rim with both hands before lifting her other foot and dipping it into the water.

I try not to watch her, but her skin is pink and faultless as she bends her knees, leaning ahead to test the murky water with all of her fingers.

"Christie!" her mother laughs outrageously. "Stop showing off."

Christie straightens, her legs on either side of her mother's waist. She touches her mother's damp hair, until Teresa sits up, smiles, and blows a loud kiss into Christie's soft belly. The child giggles, shoving steadily at her mother's head. Dropping down, she settles back on Teresa's blonde triangle of pubic hair. The hair is wet, appearing sparser and darker than usual. Christie lays her palms flat against her mother's face and turns Teresa's head one way, then the other.

"You have a kiss for me?" Teresa asks.

"Yes," Christie announces, nodding and falling forward with laughter as fresh as the splashing of water. Teresa tickles her daughter. They carry on as if I am not here at all, performing a routine, passing the soap back and forth, each one shaking her head in turn and saying, "No, you do it," until Christie finally agrees to wash Teresa. With small hands struggling to hold the bar of soap, Christie aims immediately for the sheen of her mother's weighty breasts, an expression of delightful concentration in her eyes as she carefully guides the soap along the slippery pliable skin.

The child comes up from under water. Her long hair is wet and matted to her head, her eyes jammed shut. Frantically, she rubs each closed lid, and blows droplets from her lips, before blinking and opening her mouth to breathe.

"What do you think of Kevin?" asks Teresa, speculatively eyeing me and touching her lips with one finger.

Christie squints my way and puckers her lips, mimicking her mother. Quickly she licks out her tongue at me, then laughs shrilly, kicking her feet in the tub.

"Take off your clothes," Teresa demands. "Go on, Kevin." She gestures regally with her hand. "Come on, come on. We women are curious. Do as we say. We're in control here, isn't that right, Ruler Number Two?"

Laughing, Christie nods and slips forward on her belly, suspended by her hands and by the water as she slides back and forth above her mother's legs. Her head is tilted back and she stares up at me with eyes that now seem wider because she is wet.

"Right," says Christie.

I begin to unbutton my jean shirt.

"Faster," says Teresa. "The water's getting cold. Come on."

"Faster," says Christie, giggling.

I pull my arms out of my sleeves, then undo my trousers, work them down. Stepping away from the material, one leg at a time, I stand in my underwear, waiting for further instruction. Uncertain of how far to go.

"Underwear, too." Christie says, nodding and nodding her head as she licks tepid water from her lips. She looks at her mother for encouragement. "White ones are the best. Right, Mommy? That's what you like."

My underwear slips off easily and I stand with the air fresh and cool against my skin.

"Look at that," says Teresa, pointing and winking, her mouth shaping a surprised circle. "Look, Christie. What is that? We don't have one of those."

Christie laughs. Without further words, she stands up, and holds out her hands. I walk close to her. When I am positioned beside the tub, she touches the dark soft hair along my thighs. "You've got lots of hair. You're a monkey."

"Yes," I say, not knowing what other word will please her.

"Don't be such a prude," Teresa tells me. "What's the matter with you? The look on your face! We're all just naked."

With constrained, awkward steps, Christie gradually turns around, showing me her shiny bottom as if displaying the outline of a sunburn. She gingerly touches specific places with her fingertip, playfully pressing in, her neck straining while she attempts to stare back at me.

"Kiss my bum," she says saucily. "Right there." She puts her finger on the spot. "Kiss my bum."

"That's not nice, Christie," Teresa chides. "Don't do that." She winks my way. "But you can kneel for me. We know your place. A woman always knows." Adopting a pompous tone again, she pronounces, "Down, you lowly subject. Bow down to the Queens of the Bathtubdom." She frowns with forced seriousness, and points precisely at the rug beside the tub. Christie leans her bum further out over the rim as Teresa stands stiffly from the bathtub like an empress awaiting her servant's towel, water streaming from her body.

I kneel because she wants me to. Teresa lifts her right leg and sets it on the rim, pressing her body close to my face. Christie turns to face us, wrapping both arms around her mother's left leg.

"Worship me the way it was meant to be," says Teresa, a comic tone of nonchalance slackening her manner as she stares down at me, taking hold of my head and rubbing my hair, purring out the words, "I'm an earth goddess and my body's the most natural thing. Have a good look," nudging me, pressing my face in tight to her, "closer. Yes, look at it, Kevin, taste the body. Let me see your pretty tongue."

"This is how you came to be," Teresa whispers, lowering a match to the candle. A quiet moment later, wide arcs of shadows quiver across the bedroom walls, languidly pulsing toward the dark corners. "It's a very quiet thing." Teresa carefully blows out the match, "Shhhh" and turns for me. "We're all so clean," she says, smiling so I can see her teeth and her eyes above the dimness of her naked body. "It feels so good and right to be naked and clean."

Christie sits on a chair against the far wall, her face and skin warmed by the candlelight's orange shadows. She watches the bed, leaning slightly forward to set her hands flat against the seat between her bare knees.

"Sit up, sweetie," Teresa says to me. Standing by the side of the bed, she adds, "please," and watches as I use my elbows to ease up with my back against the wicker headboard. The sheets are cool and fragrant. Teresa has sprinkled them with perfume. Enticing as they are, they provoke a placid yet steady yearning.

"It feels so beautiful," says Teresa, kindly smiling over at Christie. "Always remember how beautiful it's supposed to be. That's the only thing that matters."

"Okay," says Christie, nodding once. Rhythmically, she opens and closes her knees, as if in harmony with the lazy momentum of a song that plays in her head.

"This is it," Teresa explains, her gaze falling across my face. Savouring the stillness for a moment, she then takes a deep breath before walking around to the other side of the bed. I follow her movements as she kneels onto the mattress, one knee, then the other, up onto the sheets. She sensuously crawls toward me.

"I love you, Kevin," she says in a voice so quiet and unsteady that I know her words are true. I stare at her eyes, feel the limb-lightening spill of weakness spread inside me because of what she has said.

"Do you love me?" she asks, her tone drawing goosebumps to my flesh. With the same thrilling sentiment, she carefully touches my stomach with her warm fingertips.

"Yes," I say, and she skims her hands lower, gently stroking my penis.

"Touch my breasts," she says, arching her back slightly so that her chest rises, her breasts tightening, becoming firmer. "They used to feed the baby. My nipples. Squeeze them."

"Touch my breasts," says a small voice from the corner, the sound far away and so low it is barely audible.

I glance over and Christie smiles sweetly, but with a hint of lonely suspicion, uncertain of why she is here. Her vulnerability is like a fist grasping at my heart, each breath constrained by the power of her concern. I have to look away, stare at my hands and what they are holding, and wonder about the goodness of all that is natural.

Teresa swings one leg over my mid-section and directs my stiffening penis beneath her, taking delicate aim. Joyfully, she eases down, her shivering eyelids closing to fully internalize, and thus expand, the concentration of pleasure.

"Ohhh," she says, warmth entering her, gripping me. "Honey, it feels so beautiful. It's how we make babies." She pulls up, then down, sustaining a smooth sopping momentum, allowing the clutch of her warm sensual grip to gently guide her, careful not to break the seal.

The child pushes off her chair, and steps cautiously toward the candle, her hands holding the top of the dresser. Staring at us, then staring at the flame, she mildly blows on it, aware of how her breath makes it dance. Moments later, she turns and thoughtfully studies the orange shadows; how they flicker along our naked swaying bodies. What the colour does to us convinces her of something, assures her in a way that carefully settles her nervousness. She studies our shadows rising high along the walls, then returns to her chair and sits, observing us in silence.

Teresa sits on the edge of the bed, watching Christie and smiling encouragingly.

"Okay?" she says.

"Yes."

"That's your education for today, baby girl. Was it okay?"

Christie nods and looks where I am kneeling on the bed. My body is still, except for the rising of my chest; harsh breath drawn in and rasped out again. Beads of sweat trickle from my hairline, down across my damp forehead, before catching in both eyebrows. I press the sweat away with the butt of my palm and sit back on my heels until my legs begin to hurt. Moving them out from under me, I recline against the pillow.

"That's it," says Teresa. "A baby's in my tummy now. Kevin's semen and love and my love and egg makes the baby in my tummy; a part of him and a part of me joined like that. A little sister or brother just for you. Isn't that the most gorgeous thing ever?"

A stream of sweat creeps down Teresa's back, finding the crease of her bum. She reaches behind and swipes at the trail, but the droplets have already passed, finding their way lower. Her hair has come loose and sways freely along her spine when she turns her head. Glancing back at me, she leans slightly, stretching to carefully touch my arm, and her fingers are trembling. She smiles at me and kisses the stiff fingertips of her other hand, sets them to my lips.

"Can I do it?" Christie asks.

"You're too young," Teresa patiently explains. "It'll hurt too much and you have to really care for someone. You have to love them, very very much."

"Later," says Christie, nodding reasonably and staring at her mother's belly. "Later is okay for me, isn't it?"

"Sure," says Teresa. "If you're in love, sweetheart." She lifts her fingers away from my arm and stands. Stepping toward the candle, she watches it thoughtfully. I admire her profile as she makes a quiet, almost nostalgic, kissing sound toward her daughter, then blows out the flame.

Teresa and Christie disappear before my eyes, and there is silence for a brief but solid space of time.

"Where are you?" calls Christie, her tone vaguely frightened, but with humour struggling to remain nestled in her sweet voice. "Where?" she calls: "Mommy?"

I feel the mattress take the weight of someone's body.

"I'm on the bed," Teresa announces. "I drew the curtains. Silly-silly. It's okay. Just follow my voice. Listen... follow... follow. Reach out. Can you feel me?"

The mattress sinks slightly under a new, lighter weight and, in a matter of moments, small hands blindly touch me. I let the hands explore my body, discovering, searching the hardness of my flat chest.

"Mommy," Christie calls out in distress, "Mommy!"

"It's okay, Christie," I say, attempting to calm her. "It's just me."

"It's okay, baby," says Teresa. There is quick movement from the bed and in a second the light clicks on above us. Christie's body is close to mine, and she laughs, wiping the beginnings of tears from her eyes.

I glance toward the doorway, see Teresa standing with her hand on the light switch. The room made brilliant now, each slight movement so explicit.

Teresa takes a deep breath. "The two of you look so beautiful," she says, barely shaking her head and proudly touching her fingers to her lips.

St. John's, 1990

Two Crosses

I've seen plenty of things die. Animals. Mostly animals. First thing, I
see them sick: hobbling or falling over, then struggling up. I take care
of them. I give them food and do my best to nurse them because there's
something about saving things that just seems right.

Then they get a little better. They get real active, like everything's
coming back to them, but then I find them on the floor or in the grass,
dead.

I got used to it after a while. Living alone out here with no one
but the animals, I got used to things like that. Dying. They're just
empty. Animals are empty when they die. But people, people are a
different story. I saw a couple of them dead myself. They were out on
the lake and they didn't look empty at all. I think it's because of the
flesh. Us being the same, being made of the same thing and not
understanding how we'd be empty ourselves. Animals can be empty.
Sure. But us, I don't think so. Empty doesn't seem right. Flesh just
doesn't go that way.

The two dead people I saw were frozen on the lake. They were lost
in a blizzard. I know it. Those blizzards close in around you and you
see nothing but the white stinging and freezing your face from all
directions. I've been trapped myself. I know how you've got to push
to make it home, how you've got to cling onto something and move
away from sleep that's like a warm wind wanting to take you. I know
about that and how I could've been dead too.

One of those dead men was frozen sitting up, staring, like a kid. The
other one was on his knees with his head tucked down. They were
men, full-grown and heavy. Tough and dead like that.

The one sitting was staring toward the sky, his eyes still open when
I found him. His beard was white and hard and I touched it and grabbed

his arm to lift him but he was heavy and the arm felt like it'd snap in two if I pulled harder, so I stopped. I imagined the sound that arm would make snapping. I imagined the sound like nothing else. His fingers were the coldest, smoothest things I ever felt. But they were thick and numb like when your arm falls asleep under you. He had no mitts on. I couldn't figure that. But then I could. The other guy on his knees had two sets on his hands. What did that mean? I thought of things like love. I don't know why I thought love, but I did. I thought of that, but where was love here? Maybe they were brothers. Maybe just friends. Either way, they weren't much of anything now, mitts or no mitts.

They were on the edge of the lake and they looked alive when I first saw them. People always look alive. Just sleeping, they say.

I saw them from the window of my cabin. I stood there with a cup of tea. It was early and the sun was red coming up. I watched the colour leak across the lake and then I saw the two of them on the edge of the ice. They were facing my cabin. The one who was sitting was staring as if he could see me. I waited for them to move but they never did. I remember laughing kind of soft at first and shaking my head. I sipped some tea and it was warm. I shook my head again.

I laid the cup down and pulled on a sweater, my parka and boots, and pushed the door open. I had to put my shoulder into it to get the door through the snow outside. It opened a crack and then further until I could get my foot out. I kicked at the snow, and the door gave a little more. I squeezed out, sucking in my breath to get through.

The sun was up now and it wasn't red any more. I struggled like a new colt, knee-deep in snow, until I got to the edge of the lake. The ice was smooth and pale blue like old worn glass. The snow had blown off and there were huge banks around the edge of the lake by the dark green trees. I walked to the two men with my boots giving good traction. They were there, just the way I'd seen them first. The closer

I got to the sitting one, the more I figured he was going to say something. He was staring like he was going to ask me a question. It was like that. But I knew he wasn't going to say anything. That's what frightened me the most: knowing how his tongue was hard and frozen in his mouth, how he was never going to say anything again, ever.

I stood there considering them with the winter sun on my face and my breath puffing. I watched them like that for more than an hour. They didn't seem empty. I shook my head and looked at my bare hands and at the kneeling one with his head tucked down and his woollen cap covered with frozen snow. I studied my fingers and slowly moved them back and forth, then looked at the sitting one again. The more I watched his eyes, the more I wanted to keep moving my fingers. I had to keep them going. Otherwise, I feared they'd stop. He was staring at me and his eyes were filled with something that emptied everything out of the woods around us.

I left the bodies the way they were. Snow fell on them.

The wind came up and blew it off. A hard snow crusted over their bodies, then a white ice covered them. They were here in the middle of nowhere. What could I do? I could bury them in the snow, but the snow would melt and they'd be there just the same as always. There was no way of cutting through the hard frozen earth with my shovel blade; it would easily snap. And what good would that do anyone? So I left them on the lake and wondered how they'd gotten there in the first place. I watched them every day, wondering.

They must have come a long way.

When spring finally came round, I buried their thawed carcasses next to the animals I'd tried to save. I hammered two crosses into the ground with the back of my shovel. It took me some time to summon the words. I began reciting what I recalled of a prayer, but it was filled with holes and my whispering voice soon trailed off. I was thinking of how I didn't know what to write on the crosses. I tried to form something, but nothing offered itself. Not knowing what to do, I left the crosses blank and went back to my cabin.

No one showed up looking or asking questions.

I planted a few flowers on the graves and watched them grow; the colours were bright and healthy. When winter came again, the flowers died and snow covered the earth. I could see the two crosses there for a while, but after the third bad storm they were buried. No sign of nothing. Whiteness blanketing everything, as far as the eye could see, but I couldn't forget that those two were down there in the ground, bundled up for winter and staring straight into my head.

St. John's, 1988

The Slattery Street Crockers

Squid Crocker's feet slid and skimmed down the stairs, his left hip bumping hard while his hands grabbed for the slippery wrought-iron railing. He hit the grass-clotted asphalt at the bottom and remained where he was, sitting dazed, waiting to raise his thin long-haired head and look around.

Squid's father, Gord, observed from the top of the high stairs. He laughed like a cat, hissing through an infected throat, the tail of his t-shirt out in the front, his worn grey pants too short above his yellow socks.

"Getta fuck up," he called, laughing right on top of the words.

Squid's eyes were slow and unfocussed. Without checking his position, seemingly accepting the fall as part of what should happen, he reached out to stand.

Tammy Hynes watched from across the street, having just stepped from the Red Circle Store with a paper bag held in one arm. The sun was immediately drawn to her curly black hair and the top of her head seemed unbearably hot. She could not help but see Squid; his family's old row house was directly across from the store. "Christ!" Tammy cursed under her breath. "Some father," she griped, using her knee to hoist up the slipping bag, calling out, "Why don't you fucking help him?"

Gord Crocker's smile was slow in stopping. He squinted her way.

"Why don't you help him up?"

Gord laughed and waved in a merry way, acknowledging her presence and brushing her off at the same time.

"Crazy old man," scoffed Tammy, stepping away with resignation, her face tightening with scowl lines around her dark eyes and mouth. Thinking hard on something, her young features turned bitter and worn.

"Some old man there," she said, but she was not referring to Gord

Crocker. Her ire was intended for Squid, the father of her four-year-old son, Ricky, who watched from the row-house doorway, clutching tight to a handful of Gord's pant leg and staring blankly down the steps.

Squid made it across the street and into the take-out. Stumbling between the booths, he rammed a hand down along the back of one seat to brace himself, then shoved off toward the counter, where he stood, unsupported, lilting to the right as he dug in his pocket for the money he already had in his hand, the bills dropping to the floor, resting beside his steel-toed boot.

"Number one," he said, referring to himself when the girl in the white apron came out from behind the kitchen door to stare at him, her lips tightening with an expression of patient disgust.

"You want a number one?" she asked, waiting to call the order back through the hole.

"No, 'm number one." He smiled, his saggy eyes moist and soft.

"Yeah, right." The girl smirked, shifted on her feet. "What'd'you want, Squid?"

"Fish'n'chips." He slapped his hand against the counter, then went back to searching for his money, unable to fit his fingers into the pocket, shoving down but missing the hole each time, his fingers wiggling around outside the pocket, searching the air. He tried to look down at what he was doing but the strain seemed almost unbearable, something complicating the pull on his eyes, his sense of balance turning on him. He looked up at the girl with a confused, vacant expression.

"One piece?"

Squid nodded, his sloppy shoulder-length hair falling toward his face. He flicked back his head, dramatically, almost snapping his neck.

"Money." The girl said, laying her hand palm-up on the counter, tapping her knuckles there. "First."

Squid pressed his lips together in certainty, assuring her, nodding.

His expression relaxed and then he went through the motions again, his fingers searching, hands patting the front of his t-shirt as if he was wearing his jean jacket, until a young boy came up from behind and picked up the money, tossing it onto the counter and going back to his seat without a word.

"Hey," Squid barked, sighting the money there. He shot a stare behind him as if someone had made the mistake of challenging him.

"One piece fish and chips," the girl announced, pressing the buttons on the old register so that they clicked loudly.

Squid hobbled ahead, toward the big windows at the front of the take-out. "Hey," his tone friendlier as he walked stiff-legged toward the boy's booth and shoved in, grabbing him in a headlock and punching him weakly, laughing and coughing.

"Your change," the girl called in such a demanding way that Squid thought about getting up. But, feeling drained by the idea of going through all that again, he stopped himself, staying put, deciding he'd go up there when the food came through and tell the girl to keep the change, get in her good books, maybe get a little piece of her for being such a hero. One piece pussy and chips. He laughed to himself, shaking his head, then looked over at who was sitting with him.

"Wha's up?" he asked the boy.

"Nothing." The boy stared at his cola can resting on the table-top, then took hold of it with both hands, pressing a dent into the flimsy tin with his thumbs.

"On the pip." Squid nodded.

The boy shrugged. "I don't know."

Squid laughed once, "Fucking right." He nodded twice. "I's once."

The boy drank from his can, tipping it back, draining off the contents. Then he stared defiantly at Squid.

"Move," the boy said.

Squid shook his head, all the way one way, all the way the other, then closed his eyes, laughing harshly.

The boy ducked down, crawled under the booth and out, tossing the can in the garbage bin, its steel flap swinging in.

When Squid looked for the boy again, he was gone.

Gone.

Gone.

Gone.

"One piece fish and chips," Squid finally heard. He lifted his head from the booth and felt sick, shoved himself up and staggered toward the door, leaving his change and his order behind, forgetting completely what he was there for as he charged out into fresh air.

Tammy and her son Ricky were waiting at the bus stop when they saw Squid stumbling out of Leo's. He made it down the three concrete stairs and threw up without even bending over, the vomit flying from him in a stream while he continued walking, striding blindly out into Slattery Street where a white van screeched and hit him, knocking him down, Squid's body ramming the pavement so hard he could not hear the running footsteps nor the shrill string of screams that wildly followed.

II

Ricky stood leaning in the doorway, one hand resting snugly in the pocket of his jeans, the other hand raising a cigarette to his lips. He took a draw and sucked on the insides of his mouth, pulling together the spit that he let fly down into the street.

"Come in here," Tammy called sharply from somewhere in the dark house behind him. "Get in, or I'll break your fucking necks."

Ricky glanced back, then down at his side, checking on his little sister Patty who tottered forward with a ball in her hands.

"She's all right," Ricky called out.

"Get fucking in here," Tammy screamed, but neither of them paid attention. They simply stood where they were, watching the street, until their mother stomped out and dragged them in by their arms, slamming the door with such a boom that the wild shouts became suddenly muffled.

III

The school building was low and old, with countless rows of long windows. Inside, there was a smell of decay. Ricky pulled off his clothes in a hurry, his underwear and even his socks, then stood there with the air on him, before stepping off to wander from room to room.

In the dim outer office that led into the principal's room, he remembered the matches in his jeans pocket and went back for them.

Returning, he opened a filing cabinet and dumped piles of papers on the floor, recognizing some of the names that were typed there. He crouched among them to light a match, the flame set to each corner of paper until the hot colours grew more luscious and higher and he stood above them, beginning to feel the heat against his skin.

He thought of his teacher and went to her classroom, glanced over the students' work on the bulletin boards and the science projects on the long tables in the back. He walked with one match lit, passing on its heat, giving brightness to it all, small fires hanging from bulletin boards, flickering from tables, orange light in the darkness that gave him comfort. It was dangerous, all exciting and beautiful. It put him at total peace, the lulling violence that would not harm him as long as he kept stepping back.

IV

"We can't meet him," Tammy said, buttering a slice of toast with one side, then the other, of the knife. "Got no way down."

Ricky's sister Patty ate a mouthful of cereal, chewing and watching her mother while she pawed a dry strand of dyed blonde hair back, hooking it behind her ear. Her skin was extremely pale and made to seem paler by the bleached colour of her hair.

"You've got school, anyway. Not like this won't be the first time he got out."

Patty ate another mouthful of cereal and felt queasy, her stomach turning on her lately. She felt like throwing up, stood from the table and went up the narrow uneven stairs to the bathroom, immediately dropped to her knees, heaving and cursing between the rushes, gasping out a boy's name from up the street, cursing on him. She was not frightened about her sickness. She knew what was happening to her body.

V

"Don't you worry about it," Ricky told her, sitting on the side of her bed, feeling the need to chat with his sister before going out to reacquaint himself with the neighbourhood. "I know what you're sick from." He glanced at her face, watching her eyes fill up with tears. The sight of tears in her eyes made him feel weak and mean at once. He took a quick look at her stomach, at her hands resting there, his sister lying on top of the bed covers and daylight outside.

"You go ahead."

"And what?" Patty asked, staring at the ceiling.

"Have it."

"Mom'll kill me, Ricky."

Ricky listened for a sound downstairs. "Mom's too old for that now."

"It's Teddy Ryan's, you know that."

"I don't give a fuck about Teddy Ryan. I'm talking about the baby."

Patty began to cry with her mouth open and Ricky watched her.

"I'm on probation so I can't do nothing to him."

Patty nodded, tears spilling fat and warm from her eyes while she stared at the ceiling. "Just don't get drunk," she managed to say, wiping at her face. "You'll do it then and they'll lock you up again right away."

Ricky stood from the bed and glanced out the window at the facings of row houses across from them. He saw a man, a stranger in a t-shirt, move behind one small window. Looking back at his sister, Ricky gritted his teeth and wished there was never anything holding him back.

"I'll be the dad," he said.

VI

"Heart attack," Patty told him from her place across the table.

Ricky shook his head and stared at the toddler on his sister's knee, the toddler watching him with serious interest, the glasses on his face too big for him. Ricky tried to smile at the boy but he was thinking of his mother.

"They'll let you out for the funeral."

Ricky looked at his sister.

"They'll let me out," he said, then glanced up at the bars of fluorescent lights above them. "That fucking white light," he mumbled, setting his attention on the guard over in the corner. "You hear what I said."

The guard nodded. "Sure, Ricky."

"Joey made you a drawing." Patty offered the piece of paper which the toddler leaned forward and slapped with his palm.

"Bang," the toddler shouted.

"That's great," Ricky said, staring at the scribble. "What's it supposed to be?"

VII

The boy was five when Ricky was let out again. As soon as Joey saw him stepping from the high steel door, he ran to Ricky as if he was his father.

"Hey," Ricky said, laughing and swooping the child up into his big arms. "How ya doing, Joey?"

"Yay," Joey said, inspecting Ricky's face and smiling, watching closely, his eyes big behind the glasses, while Ricky kissed him on the cheek.

"We wanted to meet you," Patty told him, handing him his dark blue winter parka. "Hope it still fits," she said, amazed at the size of the muscles on his arms.

"Why wouldn't it?" he asked, letting Joey down to stand on the snow-crusted asphalt in front of the penitentiary door. He glanced at the coat, then handed it back. "I don't need this," he said. He took a deep breath of the sparkling winter air and gazed around at everything so naturally bright and colourful, wide open.

VIII

"Two wings and chips," Patty said, fishing her bills from the pocket of her tight jeans.

The girl stared sadly at Patty as she took the money. "Eat in?"

Patty avoided her eyes. "Yeah."

The girl rang in the amount and returned with the change, carefully handing it over. "Sorry to hear about Ricky."

Patty nodded and glanced at the girl, unable to stop the tears from clouding her eyes. The girl shook her head like she could not believe it, then stepped close to the kitchen opening to quietly call out the order. The cook in there took a moment to poke his head forward through the rectangular hole, tilting his head with a grim consoling wink. "Sorry 'bout the news, me love."

Patty waited where she was, glancing to her side at the tall cola coolers, trying not to think about Ricky, his bruised cut-up face when the police took her to identify him. Trying not to think.

The order was resting on the counter when she glanced there again, the fries stacked higher than usual. She lifted one tray in each hand, saying thanks before turning to see her son Joey, sitting in the booth toward the big front windows, his hands on a cola can, squeezing the easy tin, then shaking the hair back out of his eyes. He would not look at her when she sat, sliding a tray of food in front of him.

Angrily, he stared away toward the door, taking a drink, tipping the can all the way back, finishing it off.

St. John's, 1990

Idling Car as Seen through Fog

I stroll through the night fog, charmed by the promise of veiled opportunity; the greyness enfolding far-off objects, restricting visibility. A casual walk invigorates my thoughts, encourages purpose and focus. I pause to study houses, marvel at their unearthly stillness. Cars creep along the road to my left, passing hazily. The yellow roof light of a taxi rolls into view. Slowing, the car's orange blinker flashes to turn into the driveway before me. The cab waits for a clear break, then jerks ahead, its wheels cutting sharply, its steering column squealing. I watch it pass three feet away, catch sight of a woman in the passenger seat, her eyes fixed straight ahead. The car ambles up the long driveway and idles beside a big old house on King's Bridge Road. The driver climbs out to help the passenger with her bags. I see them as shadows where they move back down the driveway and into the fuzzy glow of the porch light at the side of the house. The driver steps inside and the taxi is left running.

I stand with my hands in my pockets, stare past the low black iron fence, watching the cab with the driver's door open, the faint yellow light in the night's greyness.

The driver steps back out and opens the trunk. He carries other parcels in, until the trunk is empty and I hear the dull thud of it shutting. The shadow of the woman stands in her doorway, welcoming the driver, speaking casual words. He enters with the final load and the porch door closes behind him. He stays in there and I wonder what they might be doing. What could be keeping a cab driver so long in a rich woman's house?

Moving through the warm fog, I wander up the broad driveway, seeing, but knowing they cannot see me. Only light cast around the object makes its centre visible. I am near the powder-blue taxi. I wait a moment, pausing to brace the clutch of anticipation. I shift nearer, consider the open driver's door, then climb in and soundlessly shut the door. Revelling in the velour plushness of new upholstery, I run my fingers along the edge of the seat, then click the smooth gearshift down to D.

Rolling. Buttery suspension. I veer around the grassy island in the centre of the driveway.

The street is clear yet clandestine. I cruise beneath the shifting line of street lamps overhead; how they glow through the fog, the trees like shadows of themselves, their barren wet branches disappearing up higher where the lights from the street lamps dissolve away.

My calm thoughts are interrupted by the staticky call of the dispatcher, "Anyone around Torbay." I reach down and switch off the volume.

Headlights drift toward me on the opposite side of the road; how they illuminate and blur the greyness around their bright circles. A red light and then the gradual left that leads downtown; someone will be waiting for a taxi cab. An easy pick-up. They even lurch out to catch my attention. Just like that, waving you down as normal as anything and stepping toward you, *wanting* in.

The traffic on Water Street is slow-moving. It takes a few minutes to make it onto George. The car cruises leisurely along the crowded thoroughfare, a line of cabs in front of me, a few others coming up behind.

I pull over by a hot-dog vendor and park, scanning the bar signs up and down George. Through the passenger window, I see an anxious female face leaning close. The young woman taps on the glass, makes motions that suggest she needs to be taken somewhere. I patiently nod her a welcome. She opens the door and climbs into the back seat while two other young women squeeze in there, one on either side of her.

"Three, sixty-eight Freshwater Road," the first woman sharply announces.

I tip my eyes toward the rear-view to see them laughing and talking loudly. My eyes linger on their reflections. I check out what they're wearing, the make-up on their faces, the differences in height and hair colour.

The first young woman does most of the talking; the others shriek and— trying to contain themselves— finally spit out laughter. They fill the close air with an appetizing smell of liquor, perfume and cigarette smoke.

When I arrive at their address, the first young woman says, "This is it, my new place." The others lean to catch sight of the house, squinting through the fog. "Now, I just need a new man." Uncontrollable laughter bursts out while they bargain among themselves, working to come up with the fare. Once the dollars have been gathered, the first young woman hands them over the back seat to me.

"Keep it," she says, giving me a smart little smile, but I know she doesn't mean it. She has no interest in a person of my sort.

The three young women move in through the basement door. I make a mental note of the address, wait for them to get safely inside, then file away my thoughts before carefully driving off, back toward downtown. But I stay up above the hill. A taxi cab you can keep for only so long, marked the way that it is.

I pass the stone towers of the Basilica, the white glowing statue out front, continue straight onto Military Road, the expanse of black trees hiding in the grey haze of Bannerman Park. I catch a glimpse of the shadows of people shifting around in there, one of them standing still with a dog on a leash.

Once beyond the pizza place, I pull in ahead of a few cars parked beside the Fountain Spray store. Climbing out, I take a breath, regard the old archives building across the street, its pillars looming through the fog beyond its wide walkway. Watching the building with its dim high steps and columns, I notice a blue police car pass in front of me. It just keeps on going, the two officers inside talking up a storm.

I step up into the brightly lighted store: many colourful things to choose from, and so I take my time selecting exactly what I'm in the mood for.

"Four-sixty," the clerk declares, once I've laid out my snack.

Handing over the bills, I watch her face while she returns my change and fills the bag. She is a real person. She has that look to her, like she is not concerned with anything other than the simple facts of living her life. I have an urge to reach out and touch her face, trace her features with my fingertips, memorize the crevices of her lips.

"Thanks." I nod admiringly, offer the enticing hint of a smile.

Outside, the taxi idles three cars back. Two cars idle in front of it. One of them has a woman sitting in the passenger seat. She pops open the glove compartment and shoves things around in there. The other car— a new burgundy Taurus— sits empty. I stroll around to the driver's side, climb in and faultlessly cruise off. Classical music is playing from the tape deck and so I assume the car belongs to the elderly gentleman in the store who was setting bottles of flavoured mineral water on the counter. The sound of the music is urgent, practically violent, mounting and clashing toward a crescendo that I feel a part of for a moment before I have to switch it off.

I dig around in my paper bag, tear open the clear plastic wrapper on my apple flip, then pop the tab on my frosty tin of cola, leaving the sub sandwich for later. I eat and sip, aware of the muddled headlights coming toward me until I sight another church and take a right down onto Duckworth. I drift toward the row houses on Gower, head back up toward Rawlin's Cross, through the intersection, peeking at the billboard on the side of a building, but I can't make out the exact image, only the vagueness of a woman's face, her expression suggesting a proposition of some sort.

I approach Churchill Square, one of the richer sections of town, upper-middle-class slice of life. Lots of pretty high-end shops. The drug mart there stays open until midnight, the clientele always dressed in comfortable new clothes. Plenty of disposable income to toss around.

Out on the concrete walkway, I am thrilled to notice how the burgundy Taurus appears so shiny and sleek beneath the lights spilling from the drug mart's big plate-glass windows. I stand near the glass and chew up the remainder of my apple flip. I tip the cola tin way back to wash down the pastry, keeping my eyes on the idling Taurus. Then I scan the row of cars parked side by side with their noses in toward the line of meters.

A silver VW pulls into the single vacant space, two cars over from mine. A thin woman with wire-rimmed glasses leans out, shutting her door and glancing back at her headlights— seemingly preoccupied— while she wanders into the drug mart.

She's left her car idling. A car idling so close to a doorway. What could possibly happen?

I toss my wrapper and tin into the concrete waste-basket on the sidewalk and turn to search the plate-glass window. The woman has moved deep down one of the bright-white aisles.

It takes only a second to familiarize myself with the controls of the VW. Backing out, I sense that the seat is still warm, lovely, but set too close to the pedals. I reach for the bar beneath the seat, tug it up and slide my position back. The woman has left the radio set on a golden oldies AM channel. The song that's playing spins out an overly indulgent twang of nostalgia. A car freshener dangles from the rear-view: a group of fluffy kittens playing with wool. It smells wretched and I snatch hold of it, snap the thin string and toss it out my window.

The fog appears to be thickening, and I remember how I forgot my sub sandwich in the Taurus. The mere thought of it makes me hungrier than before, the hunger strengthening around the absence, until I am compelled to turn around.

I park the VW one street behind the drug mart at the rear of Churchill Square, and stroll back into the appeasing lights of the u-shaped complex. The idling Taurus becomes more and more obvious as I near. I open the door, lean in, snatch the bag and straighten to see the thin woman with wire-rimmed glasses standing outside the drug-mart doorway. She is staring straight at me, baffled.

"Something the matter?" I ask, keeping my tone level.

"My car," she says, hiking her purse strap up on her shoulder. "It was just right here."

"Are you sure?"

"Yes, of course, I'm sure." She points with her free hand— the one not holding the drug-mart bag— to the parking spot that another car now occupies.

"Was it a VW?"

"Yes."

"Silver?"

"Yes," her nervous voice rises. She fingers the frames of her glasses, jiggles them up higher on her nose, her cheeks flushing.

"I saw a little guy drive off with it." I lift the sub out of the bag and peel back the cellophane, make a motion to take a bite, but then stop myself, knowing I should at least attempt to sound more urgent, bump up the pace, if this is to work out as I have imagined.

"I can't..." She stumbles back, confused, plummeting through shock. "What?"

"A guy with red hair, little scrawny guy. He was wearing a baseball cap. Dirty-looking. Almost a kid. Just left. See those taillights?" I point to the farthest car in the distance, its shape obscured by the fog.

The woman squints in the general direction.

I toss the sandwich back into the bag, fling the bag into the Taurus. "You better call the police. No, he'll be long gone by then."

The thin woman stands there with the red and white drug-mart bag dangling from her hand. Again, she pushes back the thin strap of her purse.

"You want me to go after him?" But I answer the question for her. I decide by leaning into the Taurus. "That's it. I'll go after him. Find out where he is."

"I'd better call the police." The thin woman spins, then stops abruptly. "No, I'd better go..." She looks at me, straightens her glasses, her voice shivering, her skin charmingly white. "I'd better..."

"Come on, hurry." I reach across the seat and pop open the door. Such worried eyes, so uncertain.

I begin to back out. Momentum. It drags people along. The energy compels her to spring ahead toward the open door. She slides in, breathing, shuts the door, breathing... And we are moving, drifting, with the strange closeness of this woman beside me.

"He took a right on Elizabeth Avenue."

The woman says nothing, is anxious, her thoughts crackling with images of stolen cars, flashes of televised violation. She will not regard my face. I can see through the corners of my eyes that the woman is already avoiding me. This close and she is *avoiding* me.

"You can't see anything," she says, tensed by the explicitness of my body next to hers, the fog in the massive parking lot beyond the windows.

I lay my hand to rest on the moulded plastic between our seats, then floor the accelerator until I reach the edge of the lot. Taking a sharp right, I race off, tires screeching. The woman steadies herself from where she was leaned against her door.

"See," I call, pointing at the red blur of taillights disappearing around a corner at the intersection far up ahead. "That's it. Him." I shoot a convincing glance at the thin woman and she finally considers my face, wondering who I might be.

"We'll catch up," I insist. Her eyes blink unsteadily behind those delicate glasses; her tongue comes out to briefly wet her lips. The thin woman swallows.

I begin to slow, let my foot rise a touch from the accelerator.

"What's the matter?" she asks.

"I don't know. It does that sometimes. Carburetor or something."
We come to a near standstill.

"Talk about bad timing," I gripe. "Needs a tune-up."

"He's getting away," she says.

I discreetly press the accelerator, "Ah, there, that's better." I smile at her, give her a wink, then follow the path that takes us back to where I know her VW is parked. I ease up on the gas as we approach the idling car and pull up beside it. I carefully lean across the thin woman's body, catching the pleasant scent of her warmth as I strain nearer to the passenger window, wipe off the faint mist that has fogged from her breath, feel it smearing across my palm.

"Is that it? Yours?"

The woman watches through her window. "Yes," she says, exhaling with luxurious pleasure. "God, it is." She sets her palm against the place above her heart, and I stare at how she keeps it there. She is relieved, accepting, watches me as I straighten away from her. She is happy now, smiling, fortified by the knowledge that her car has been returned to her, newly trusting me with the deal safely done.

"We found it," she gushes.

"Great!" I exclaim, edging ahead to pull over in front of her VW. The thin woman immediately jumps out.

"No, no," I say, bolting after her, "wait," blocking her path so that she switches back to startled. "He might still be here."

The woman's eyes blink behind those fragile frames.

"Don't move," I command. "He might be somewhere near." Checking the area around her car— while she remains by the side of the burgundy Taurus— I search the interior of the VW, carefully scan the back seat.

"Everything seems fine," I tell her as I lean out. Smiling reassuringly, I shut the driver's door.

"Great," she says confidently, stepping near me to pass. "Thanks so much."

"You were lucky."

"Yeah." She laughs in a mock worried way and blows a breath up at her bangs. "I guess so."

"Anything could have happened."

She nods, reaches for the door handle and pops it open. But then she just stands there holding the top frame of the window.

"Someone out for a joyride," I explain. "You make sure nothing's missing. Driver's license or registration, anything like that with an address on it. Anything like that in there?"

"No," she says. "I have my purse. I hope it's..." She lifts it off her shoulder, pulls the zipper along the top. Searching around, she discovers her wallet, opens it and checks her driver's licence, her address plainly printed there. "Yes, it's here."

"Excellent," I say.

"Well..." She stares down into her purse, putting her wallet to rest.

"Thanks again for this."

"You were lucky." I take a glance around the foggy street. No cars coming in either direction. No sounds of footsteps. Nothing except the two of us.

The thin woman stands in the open doorway of her car, looking at me as if she owes me more than she is capable of giving, a sense of obligation making her final goodbye newly difficult for her.

"It was a pleasure," I tell her.

"Anyway," she says, bending into her seat and smiling up at me as she settles. I hold the open frame of her door, hold it firmly in place with both hands as she checks out the rear-view. When she spots the red string dangling there, her lips tighten slightly, but she passes no comment.

I wait for her eyes to find me again, then I gracefully, obligingly shut her door, bowing to her. I stand there watching from the other side of her window, her curious eyes staring up. What she gives me is an appreciative smile, then backs away as I raise my wiggling fingers.

Driving off, she toots her horn twice. I read her license plate, watch the blur of red taillights melding into grey, then I climb back into my idling car, and drive away, too.

Burnt Head, 1996

The Plastic Superman

It was no fault of Susie's that she was born with one grey sickly-looking eye. The other one was blue and clear as water; always shiny too, as if sunlight were flashing off it. She liked to stay at home, never wanted the outside, maybe because of the sun and her only good eye; the way it was— maybe the sun seemed twice as bright. That blue one was sensitive. I knew from the doctor.

When I took her to the clinic, the doctor always checked her hands, made sure they could move okay, because both thumbs never made it out with her when she came. That's the way me and June looked at it. After we got over the first shock of seeing her hands like that, and we got past the fear, finally realizing that Susie was just like anyone else— except for the one eye and the thumbs— then we'd pretend with each other that Susie's thumbs were still inside of June. They never made it out. Maybe the next baby would have them; be born with Susie's thumbs. It was interesting and it was funny, too. It was our way of dealing with things, the only way of really looking past everything that was trying to knock us back.

Susie's just like any other little one who's four years old, only better. She's got this smile that makes you want to grab her up from where she's sitting and hug her so hard until she starts laughing the way she does, like a funny hiccup running right after itself. When she turns her head extra far— straining to see with her good eye— her smile comes free and wide as soon as she recognizes you.

"Daddy," she says, raising her hands for me to lift her up. She has trouble standing on her own because of her foot— the missing one that throws her balance off. The doctor said they could do something about that later, so I don't give it much mind. He told me they'd put a foot on the end of her leg where the foot should be. It'll look just like the other foot; the real one, he said.

If she has to, she can manage getting up on her own, but she likes to have me lift her anyway. She says it makes her dizzy the way I hoist her up so fast and high, hold her above my head, press her to the ceiling and laugh at her wild chuckling. Every now and then the pain cuts into me from my back, but Susie's so light— but getting heavier— and I'll have to stop lifting her soon and pay attention to what's getting worse in my spine.

Without fail— when she's up there at the ends of my arms— Susie always reaches down to poke her finger into the hole where my front teeth used to be. Her little fingers like rubbing over my gums until it tickles too much and I've got to jerk my head away. Those front teeth got shattered to little spitting bits when a beam of steel swung loose and hit me in the face, knocking me backward and down two storeys where my spine took the worst kind of smack against a stack of gyprock.

Lucky to be alive, they told me, but I needed no such convincing. I thank the Lord every day for sparing me, so I can be here to look after my family.

That accident happened six years ago and I can't ever work at labour again. Without labour work, there's nothing for me. The construction company wouldn't give me any money, because I was working for cash under the table to make a few extra dollars while I was on unemployment insurance. So, I couldn't get any compensation and I couldn't sue the company because I shouldn't have been there in the first place. Their insurance wouldn't cover it. They said it could put them out of business if it got around.

The company told me to sign a piece of paper saying it wasn't their fault and they wouldn't report me to the unemployment people about my working illegally. I had to do it. With a family to look out for, I didn't want them thinking I was a crook in the newspapers. June and me and Perry— God rest his soul. Perry got leukemia and went away to nothing but a pair of small slow-moving eyes rolling over to stare at us as if we were the ones he didn't want to recognize the most, like he wanted us to go away because the sight of us was more painful than the hurt of what that horrible disease was doing to his insides. But he'd make himself smile all the same, force the smile and try to say how much he loved us and... I can't think of what went on. My bones ache when I think of Perry, like they can feel the cold of where he's buried.

Two years after the accident, June told me real soft in the dark one night. She said, "There's a baby in me, Bren," and I felt like my smile was glowing when I heard the news. A little baby to wash away all the black regrets that Perry's death had stained us with. I could feel those regrets sticking to me, caked on my skin so sometimes it felt like my body was sealed up and I couldn't even sweat.

And then came Susie.

Chris from down at work told me what was happening with the other guys that were working there illegally, too; kids were being born with missing parts just like Susie. Something was on the construction site, Chris told me. A poison that you couldn't see was melting down God's blessed work. And nobody could do anything about it because we weren't supposed to be there in the first place. All of us working for under-the-table cash.

Chris told me they closed the building after and were thinking on tearing it down altogether. He told me the television and radio news people were calling and showing up at his house, wanting to talk to him because news was around about the trouble. The doctors at the hospital got together and agreed that certain wrongful things were happening to the children that were much alike. Chris told me the news people were after him, but he wouldn't talk. I can't see anyone talking about what happened. What's there to do now but face what's right in front of you and be thankful for the blessings easily seen if a person is willing to take a good look at the plentiful miracles in this world?

June works washing dishes at a small restaurant downtown. They don't pay much— lower than the minimum wage— but it's all cash and it never affects our welfare which we can't live on anyway. The good thing about the restaurant is that they let June take home the leftover cooked food at the end of the day, if she's working the late shift. If it's in the morning, then there's plates that come back from the restaurant tables that aren't even touched, so June can take that food home if she wants to.

Ms. Rose— her boss— is always glad to help out like that. They serve strange-tasting food down there, but they told June it's good for you and, not only that, it doesn't cost one red cent. So some of our food comes without a problem. Not a worry except we have to be careful because after the food sits around on the counter down there for a while it can do terrible things to your stomach.

I was in the emergency four or five times already for food poisoning. The heat in the restaurant kitchen makes the food go bad fast— no room in their refrigerator for leftovers— so we have to be careful.

Emergency takes me in and lays me down on a clean white bed and draws some blood from me. They check my temperature and put that black rubbery strap around my arm, pump it up to see if my blood pressure's okay.

A couple of times they kept me there overnight because my fever was so high and my blood cells were out of whack. I was so weak from throwing up and running to the bathroom with everything streaming out of me at both ends that I welcomed the thought of being treated so nice by all the nurses and doctors.

June just gets a little bit of stomach sickness. That's the worst it hits her— going to the bathroom over and over— but she doesn't get the violent heaves like me, with my face and neck like they're going to explode from the pressure of trying to retch something up from a stomach that's already empty. Susie never gets touched by it at all. It's like she's got some special strength that makes her solid and protects her from any kind of harm; maybe her own perfect angel watching over her, taking the place of the parts that're missing.

She's like the little superman that she plays with. The plastic one I gave her. He's painted blue with the red "S" and red trunks. Only five inches tall and his hard legs move back and forth. Arms, too. And his rust-coloured boots come off. One of his hands is tightened up into a fist and the other one is halfway closed, the fingers curved like he's about to grip hold of someone for doing an evil deed. It's a sloppy job, the flesh-coloured paint that's on them hands. Tiny little hands for a superman with fingers that don't move. And his chest muscles are pushing out in thick layers showing everyone that he can handle any size of thing that gets in his way. There's a red plastic cape, too, stiff and clipped into holes in his shoulders. You can pull off the cape and see superman without his flying powers. He looks like some kind of weird-dressed clown without his cape, just standing there waiting for something to happen, for someone to lift him up and guide him into the sky.

Susie holds him between her middle and index fingers, and streams him through the air over her head. When her arm gets tired, she stands the plastic superman in her short, sandy-blonde hair, sliding his feet around in her curls.

"Superman's walking on the top of the world," she tells me, tilting her head to one side and making a silly face.

"He's looking for bad guys," I say, leaning on the wall, wanting to sit next to her but afraid of the quick coming of pain in my back.

"On the look-out."

"Superman saves people," Susie tells me, her blue eye flashing light as her smile opens up, showing me two rows of the whitest teeth I've ever seen. "He saved me from the monsters who bit off my thumbs."

I gave Susie the superman when she was two years old. Bought it down on Maxie Street where a little chubby kid was selling off all his toys.

He had a table on the sidewalk and it was covered with plastic figures: grey dinosaurs, green and red mutant creatures, soldiers, different coloured animals— pigs and farm cows. A big teddy bear was there, too, sitting up on a cardboard box. They wanted five dollars for it.

The woman with the chubby kid was skinny and had thick reddish-grey hair that looked like a shag rug. She had an old face with a few white whiskers growing from her chin. Thin as my finger she was, the white short-sleeved blouse hanging off her. It was a slippery material with little blue triangles on it. She was wearing brown corduroys and stood by the boy selling her dishes, old-looking dishes: cups and saucers that seemed delicate but were kind of yellow because they'd been around for a long while.

I stared at the teddy bear, then touched to see how soft he was. He was soft as anything, almost warm with the memories that I knew were in him. There was a little bit of cardboard taped on his light brown fur with the price that made me hungry just reading it. Five dollars.

An old man was standing by the kid's table. He just shuffled up close to me and stood by my side, staring down at the table then glancing sideways at me. His black baseball cap was resting high on his head. He had on a heavy brown suit jacket that looked like it weighed too much for him to be carrying on his shoulders, and thick woollen trousers despite the heat. He was grey-faced and slow, grunting as he fingered through the small pile. I saw the superman in there and took hold of it, almost afraid to ask for the price. My eyes were quick as they went over the hard figure and they were fast to find out that it was in perfect shape.

"How much for the superman?"

The chubby kid looked down into his tray of silver coins, and said, "Five cents."

I smiled and reached into my pocket to show him that I had sixty-seven cents, but he wasn't interested. I gave him the nickel and kept poking through the pile. The old woman came over and started digging out quarters, dimes and nickels, counting up the right change for a dollar minus five cents.

"Here you go," she said, handing me the coins.

"No," I told her. "I only gave him a nickel."

"Oh," she said, blinking at me and squinting as she leaned her head close to my lips. "What?"

"I gave him a nickel."

"Yes," she said, her thin fingers taking their time to drop the money back into the red tray. She nodded and stepped close to her dishes. Slightly stooped forward, she watched the passing cars, waiting for an offer.

The chubby kid looked up and stared at me like he finally recognized what it was that I had in my hand.

"Superman," he said, throwing his stumpy arms up over his head and laughing.

Susie throws her hands into the air now, too, like she's going to take off and fly. June is in the living room with her body laid out on the couch. She's sleeping after working day and night, but there wasn't much food left over because they were busy and everyone ate what they ordered. It was a hungry day, June says about times like this, like everyone else was too hungry, eating the food that was supposed to be ours, and now we're hungry instead.

"Shhh," I say to Susie. "Mommy's sleeping."

"Okay," says Susie, lowering her arms and dropping the superman, but then raising those arms again for me to take hold of her.

I bend and lift her from the carpet. When my back tightens, shoots of pain spark out into my neck and head and down my legs like the pain's been sent by wires, by someone flicking a big switch. I almost lose hold of Susie, my hands going weak. I lay her back down with a thud and drop to my knees.

"What's wrong?" Susie asks, watching my face with her quick head tilted to the side, letting her shiny blue eye do the work of two. "Daddy?"

"It's okay," I say, my teeth grinding together.

She takes the plastic superman and bends him at the waist, bends his knees and sets him down by my side, so he looks just like me. I watch the figure and hear a knocking at the door, making me edge over to the wall and brace it with my hands to get up slowly so I don't pass out.

Susie pushes with all of her fingers, pressing them hard into the carpet and bending her back to stand up. It takes her a little bit of struggling to get to her feet but she manages okay, then limps off toward the door where I hear her opening it at the end of the hallway.

"Yes," she says, then she shouts right away, "DADDY."

I'm watching June, hoping she won't wake up. But she does, and sighs, rolling onto her other side before raising her head and listening, then sighing as she sets her feet on the carpet and sits up real slow.

"What?" she says, softly coughing once.

"The door," I tell her.

She sits straighter, rubs her nice-looking face, only starting to get a few wrinkles around the eyes, and yawns before standing and going to answer the door like it's automatic.

"Who is it?" she asks, passing me.

"I don't know, but Susie's got it."

Chris pokes his head into the living room just as June takes the corner. She stops suddenly, nods at Chris, then leans out to peek down the hallway, calling for Susie.

"I'm here," Susie says, hobbling forward.

Chris shakes his round crew-cut head. His chin is tucked in and I see his double chin is getting bigger. He's wearing green work pants and a green shirt. His hands are in his pockets like they always are and he looks like he doesn't remember what he came here for, standing there, moving some change around in his pocket while he watches me head toward the couch.

"What's going on?" I ask, carefully sitting, tightening up my muscles so the pain won't touch me. But the pain always touches me anyway, no matter how tightly I hold onto my insides.

"The television," Chris says, pulling up the old vinyl foot stool and plunking down as it disappears under him. "They got talking to some of the boys about the Rex Building." The words make him stop and he rubs his eyes good and hard with the butt of his palm. When he looks at me again, the skin around his eyes is gone pink. "We were working illegally, but the television people don't care. They say it doesn't matter. They're giving good money just in case the unemployment people come after us. Covering our butts. We can pay them back. It's like that. But the government won't do anything because they should've known better anyway and inspected the building better. They can't do a thing 'cause they're just as guilty as anyone."

"So you went along with it," I say, knowing by the way he's talking that they got to him. The way he's talking, trying to convince me, I know he's part of it.

"The money they gave me. I can't say how much because they told me not to, but it's plenty. You want me to tell you? I don't care. I'll tell you. What're they gonna do?"

I glance at the entranceway to the living room and see June standing there, holding Susie up against her body. Susie's got her legs wrapped around June's waist and her arms wrapped around June's neck and she's kissing her mommy again and again on the cheeks; one, then the other, then the first one again.

"Can you take her upstairs?" I say, nodding so my wife understands that we're talking about things Susie shouldn't hear.

"Sure," says June. "It's bed-time soon anyway." She lowers her face close to Susie's and smiles, lifting her eyebrows. "Right?"

"No," says Susie, slowly shaking her head. "No way. Not going. Uh-uh."

June steps over to us. "Kiss Daddy good night." She tips down and I kiss Susie on her little lips, take hold of her fingers and feel them in my hand, the happy way they hold onto me.

"And Uncle Chris," says June.

"Night, beautiful," says Chris after kissing her. He wipes his lips with the back of his green sleeve because Susie can be a real wet kisser.

June smiles at me before leaving, closing her heavy eyelids and opening them again to let me know she's going to bed herself. I wave at Susie and wait 'til they're gone before setting my attention back on Chris.

"What about being a criminal?" I ask him. "You got family, too. They'll find out about that."

Chris edges closer on the foot stool and whispers kind of loudly, "They were the criminals. Mr. Thistle and his company. They knew about this crap in the soil. They knew it all along. That's what the television people are saying. They didn't give a damn about us."

"So."

"It's money for my family, for Sammy. To get him things he needs to fix him up. They got plastic stuff. Plastic hands and feet to put on him. Plastic ears so he looks normal."

"But Sammy's the same, anyway. Susie's the same. What difference does that plastic stuff make to anyone?"

"The money. You can get Susie some thumbs that she should've had in the first place."

I stand quick and turn away from him, hiding the pain. I stare through the small square window in the front of the house. An old woman is standing across the street, looking one way, then the other. She's using one of those metal walkers, leaning on it with her hands, moving it an inch to the left, an inch over to the right, but walking nowhere. An ambulance rolls down the street in front of her with no sirens going. It slows down, but speeds up again after a second or two.

"I didn't mean for it to sound bad, Bren. She's fine with no thumbs. I didn't mean nothing, all right. I'll tell you I'm sorry 'cause I know how you feel. I feel the same." I hear him shifting around on the foot stool because the vinyl is sticking to his legs. He's sweating right through his pants. He shifts some more, the sticky sound like he's peeling something away, then he starts talking again. "It happened to me, too. To Sammy, all right. I'm just telling you about money. You could use some money. I could use it. I'm sick of getting money under the table and doing jobs for less than minimum wage because the welfare's not enough and the unemployment's not enough. I'm sick to my stomach of it."

I can't help shaking my head, trying to deny it while I watch the old woman shuffling. A real thin string of spittle hangs down from her old lips. It swings back and forth as she inches herself along.

All the doors of the row houses are closed, and the faded drapes are pulled shut in the small windows, like everyone's hiding from something that's sure as hell going to get them, but they don't know what it is and when it's going to show its true frightening self.

"Just let it rest," I tell him. "It's no one's business what I had to do to make a buck so Perry could get some better help when he was sick. His own room and all. Other kinds of drugs. I'm still paying the bills."

"Well, they should know everything. And I'll tell them."

His words make me turn real fast. "Don't you tell them nothing about me." I point at him, trying to hold in the pain in my back that rips into me from spinning quick.

Chris pushes up from the stool, standing as if to be on guard, "I won't tell them nothing about you. I'll just take my money. You can have some if you need it. For some bills or for Susie. I want to get some stuff for Susie."

"I don't want nothing from you, nothing from anyone." I stare at him and he swallows hard and stares at the floor with tears rising in his eyes so that I've got to tell him in a quieter voice, "You got to take care of yours. You got your own to worry about."

"I got enough to take care of mine, too," he says without looking up. "That's the kind of money. It's good money. It's money like we were owed and are finally getting, only it's coming from the television people and a book writer, too, because they're the ones who want the truth." He takes a peek at me.

"They just want some garbage, Chris. That's all they want."

Chris stares back at the carpet and moves his hands in his deep pockets. Change jingles around in there. He looks up like he wants me to be his friend again, but I can't take it that way. It's all wrong and won't do any kind of good.

"Just don't mention me," I say, glancing over at the old picture of me, June and Perry that's framed in strips of lacquered wood on the wall. There's a little clock set into the corner of the picture and the second hand ticks around in circles.

"The truth, and money for it."

"And jail for the truth," I add. "I already lost too much."

Chris's eyes go a little wide and he's surprised, "Who said anything about jail?"

"It was a crime, wasn't it?"

Chris doesn't say a word.

"People look at us like we're bums, like we're illegal and ruining their lives. And they're right. It's illegal, but it's not our fault."

"It's just the truth," Chris says, pushing both hands deeper into his pockets. "Come off it. Who'd ever put us in jail for telling the truth?"

Susie is sleeping by the time Chris leaves. I know because she's not calling out or moving around in her bed. I can hear every sound going on upstairs. The walls and floors let me know. They're as thin as cardboard.

There's a strange feeling in me knowing that Susie's sleeping upstairs and she's okay. A nice feeling to know she's maybe dreaming and nothing can happen to her when she's sleeping with that soft smile on her face. I'll go upstairs and give her the superman so she can have him when she wakes up first thing in the morning the way she likes to have him.

I pick up the superman from the carpet where Susie was playing with it. His face is painted that weird flesh colour and his eyes are white and staring straight ahead. He's got a look on his face like nothing could ever bother him. The look says he's better than anyone else and he knows it. A good-guy, handsome kind of smile. The cape is off and on the carpet, so I pick it up between my toes and clip it back on.

I can't help but think of what's going to happen with Chris and the television, and I'm scared for everyone in this house. I have to say a prayer to the Lord to give me strength. If the world and the people who know how to run it have their way, they'll take me out of here and lock me up for the terrible things I've done.

June steps into the kitchen where I'm getting some water by the sink. She steps in close behind me wearing her flannel nightdress that used to be her mother's. She squeezes me from behind, hugs me around the waist, and I feel her warm body pressing into mine.

I sip my water, then turn around with the glass in one hand and the superman in the other. June stares at my eyes like she's searching around for something that'll make her love me even more than she already does. The smile on her face wants to grow wider, but it's perfect just the way it is.

"Susie asleep?" I ask.

"Mmm-hmmm," she says.

"I'll be up in a second."

"The bed's cold. Come on."

"You're tired, right?"

She closes her eyes to let me know that what I said couldn't be truer. Then she nods good and slow.

"Really tired," she says.

The glass of water is cold. It hurts my fingers, makes them pain like nothing else. I've got to put it down on the counter.

June knows that I'm done in the kitchen and walks on ahead of me, stepping real light and silent, then stopping to wait for me at the bottom of the stairs.

"Go on," she says, looking at my hand as I move close to her.

I stare at the little man. I'd forgotten that he was there at all. I raise him up over my head and glide him around in big funny circles, make a swooshing sound with my mouth. I've got to smile for her, even though I don't feel it in me.

June laughs real low and turns to hold the wooden bannister. She leans forward and takes the stairs one at a time.

"My legs weigh a ton," she says.

"Go on. Get 'em up there." I follow her steps, moving in close to her so I can smell the nightdress.

"Susie told me she doesn't like Uncle Chris," June says as she goes up, but she doesn't look back to see what I'm thinking. "She doesn't want to kiss him any more."

"Okay," I say, but I don't say anything else. Tired and climbing the stairs, I get this weird feeling like nothing's even moving.

"Sleep," June says, turning at the top of the stairs. She takes my hand and waits 'til I'm closer to her body, then leads me over to Susie's door, sets her ear against it.

"Listen," she whispers, putting a finger to her lips, and I lean in there too, hold my breath to hear more clearly, the sound of Susie's sweet little voice, singing.

St. John's, 1990

Love Story for Jan

Through this progressive disease, this human malaise termed civiliza-
tion, I worshipped beauty like a dead man given one last snap at breath.
I was a peasant. I was a fucking king. I lived in the sky and bent to
swallow trees, spat out the leaves when they began to rot and clog the
pipes. I shot rivers through my veins like a clearwater junky. I was so
wise to pick nature as my habit, agony as my purifier, self-pity as my
last-chance grab at the spiritual cash.

I opened my eyes to the truth and saw that it was night. No, my
mistake— I was blind, a grinning cripple— I'd merely forgotten to
recognize my disability. "Ability," the timid corrected me. And I
grinned more widely in agreement, blinking, pupilless.

When regret came a'courting I bought flowers and dressed in my
best too-small Sunday suit, slicked back my hair and offered a toothless
smile. Regret ate me, ground my bones to powder and puffed me out.
I was dust, blown through the desert, stinging eyes and filling nostrils
with my abrasive storm of cynicism. I was a dark poet whore, pedalling
putrid flaps of skin with clever control. Metaphors were my elitist
insignia, my beaming cross of salvation, my great big plea to find favour
with the converted few. Metaphors became my comb and brush set,
my bent mirror reflecting big bold chaos. Metaphors became my
low-life, my piddly sustenance, my sloppy overcooked dinner in a
wash of booze. I twirled them like strands of hair between my fingers,
bit the ends between my teeth and sucked them in like spaghetti. My
intestines grew jealous. They expressed consternation with a muscular
wail of shit, a fitting reflection of what I was composted of.

An inquisitive soul once poked me with a penknife and the stench
filled the world for four weeks, clouding weather and keeping the
children locked indoors. They thought it was war.

It was.

I brought together continents and spit them apart with the slaver of oceans. From there, I learned of division, separation, segregation. Nature taught me to be ashamed of myself, to be apart, to feel ill at ease. I raped it as retribution. When it rained, I laughed out mocking thunder. Lightning was my disquieting deja vu. It struck me still. I was there before, present in that brilliant shock of light, but sustained. Not a hint of the possible, but a mishmash of possibility intensified.

I was a dwarf when I died, a giant when I was born. My mother was an ancient goddess from whom people turned away once the favours ended, once the threshold was tripped over and mythologies repackaged, sporting the chic martyr disguise. Technology made her an anachronism, made currents of everything. Magic became steel. Magic became electronics. Magic became weaponry. To change and move and kill with the presto-push of a button/trigger. A quaint proposition, all dressed in lintless outfits and absentmindedly annihilating each other behind our backs.

I lived in a female stranger's open wound, I was so boyishly hurt. I felt at home. When the prognosis was described and the limb theatrically severed, I thumped to the ground and writhed out, gurgling mad. The first woman I tried to make love to, I never entered, merely touched the skin alive. I could not make love with her because the face was not shaped by the features I adored. I found the true one later, her eyes in the dark weakening me, coaxing warm tears to my eyes as I brushed her hair back along her temples and gently moved in and out of her body. But that ended.

That ended.

And the love of loss began.

I became a monster. But I was made human first. Creator's black X now lashed across my soul. Lavishly, I accepted the beauty in the world. I was the dying man who witnessed matter burst alive in a shriek of striking colour. Only through battered eyes did the world begin to change, to disclose its delicate wonder.

I leapt through love with a hollow man's weakness propped up as an anarchist's growl. No.

I stumbled.

Each negligent thrust of words deceived me into believing. I foraged forgiveness from each second-hand thought I clumsily bolted together, learning how the obvious and apparent meant nothing in the consummate stillness of the soul.

It was then that I forgot what it was. What I needed, I remembered.

What I wanted, I would say so simply, in the truer, honest pitch of a trembling child's whimper: if you see Jan, tell her this is every bit of how I feel for her.

Vancouver, 1994

Small Ones Disturb the Biggest

I left the force because the feeling of the boy against my arms when I cut him down was too much for me, the lightness of his body making the world tip way off balance. It brought to mind this doctor I knew— a surgeon named Lee Crowley— who couldn't touch a bleeding child. It scared the hell out of him when he was doing shifts in emergency; the stretcher rolling in, only partly filled, rolling faster and then stopping beneath his hands.

Lee was tattooed along the arms, just like me. We'd sometimes have a few drinks together, telling stories about the things we were up against. Once, he told me about a little girl who was brought in with her chest torn open by the wheels of a car (a drunk driver) and how he could do nothing but watch the little girl's face turn softer and softer until there was only a sweetness that was so pure and heart-breaking.

I can talk about anything else, but not the boy in the closet. I turn away from the picture of the boy's face, the length of his body. Instead, I try to focus somewhere else in the memory, on the walls of the dim closet where I found him, to concentrate on the old light fixture, the orb with the low-wattage bulb shining through. I can't help but always wonder why the orb never snapped under the weight of what was hanging from the other end of the rope. It should've just broken away from the gyprock that was barely holding it in place. It was such a delicate fixture, you could pop your fingers through it. But it stayed there, doing a job it wasn't made for.

I won't say another word about the boy, except that it was his tenth birthday. The cake was still on the kitchen table when I got there. I caught a glimpse of it as I was moving into the hallway, and there were candles with icing stuck to them on the boy's night table next to his unmade bed. The candles were laid out to spell the word: Y O U.

The mother was standing in the room, her voice twisted and crackling, her fingers over her mouth and in her mouth, shivering, eyes open and tight to one last look at her boy and everything else that pulled away from him; an instant of speed, away from the body of her son, before and after and all of his life in her eyes now set and facing the body that was no longer anyone.

The boy; he weighed practically nothing at all. I laid him down on the bed and his mother started sobbing loudly.

I stared at the boy. His face was the wrong colour, the colour thick and blue. It seemed impossible, and then I thought of Lee, the surgeon who had given up everything. Quit his job after seeing that girl come in the way she did. I first met Lee at a bar that everyone called The Shift. That was the bar's name when it opened its doors fifteen years ago, but the sign over the window later spelled something different. Most of the people who went there were old customers, so nobody called it by the new name. The space was a wide, dark hallway with a few tables and chairs placed away from the bar. The walls were painted a colour I could never identify because the lights were always way too low. And the patrons leaned on the bar itself, which was long and ran down the length of the wall to your left as you came in.

The Shift was set three blocks east of the hospital and three blocks west of the police station. Right in the middle. Its customers were mostly cops, and a few stray doctors who appreciated the connection with the street: information about what was happening that might bring the people into emergency, what to expect, which neighbourhoods were on edge.

Lee used to hang around nursing a drink for hours and listening, getting the forecast from us, interested in our talk about the streets; where the tension was mounting and what we were doing to try and defuse it. He was always concerned with what we were saying. After he quit, he stayed around The Shift for other reasons. He liked the feel of the place. He must've felt at home there in the middle of all the cop talk.

I often wondered how he ever ended up being a doctor. Most of the doctors coming into The Shift didn't look or act the part. They were more like us. Maybe they'd chosen their profession for all the wrong reasons. It didn't fit them, making them seem out of place in their own skins.

People were always settling in the wrong jobs by mistake. I saw it a lot in the harder areas. They didn't know what they should be doing, because they didn't understand or want to accept what they were really made of. It could take an entire lifetime just to figure out the misplacement, discover what it was that made a man feel off-centre all his life.

I made a point of not telling Lee about the boy. After I cut the boy down and the ambulance came and bagged his small body and they went away with the sirens shut down, I stood there with the mother and her mouth was turned, twisted and opening wider because the ambulance was moving so slowly, her body leaning forward and back, as if she were trying to force the ambulance along, speed it up with her momentum. I could tell she was confused. She wasn't sure if she should go along, so she waited, had to wait to tell her husband, be there when he arrived home, just like always, only their lives completely changed now, becoming something else not like their lives at all.

"Do you want me to call your husband?" I asked her. She nodded and kept nodding, but didn't say a word. Her eyes were watching me and they couldn't make any sense of the need springing around inside her.

"I'll drive you to the hospital."

"No." She shook her head, shutting her eyes, denying the whole works, not wanting to accept it as hers.

I stayed with her because I thought it was the right thing to do, but when she clamped onto me, throwing her arms around my shoulders, finally bursting out with real noise in my ear, I didn't want to stay there any longer. She was holding closer and I felt her lips pushing into my neck and then her smooth teeth pressing carefully, then harder against my skin. Her tongue was there, too. It was wet and thick and slow, and her chest was bucking with quick shallow sobs. Her mouth opened wider. I felt her lips moving and her teeth started digging into me, biting, so I stepped back away from her to leave her where she was, watching me.

I drove away, looking in the rear-view at the woman standing in the doorway, her tiny shivering reflection. The distance between us was too much and I was losing that last shred of what was keeping me together, my self-control starting to splinter and prick me before flitting away, like that woman's need, into the space between us.

I drove on and was home before I realized I was actually moving. I changed my clothes. Then I went to the station with my uniform balled up in a plastic bag on the back seat. I parked the patrol car and glanced at the seats and at the floor, then stared at the radio, counting and saying to myself, "If I get a call, just let it happen." I was gritting my teeth, feeling some wicked strength was going to tear me in two. "Tell me, I'll take one more call. One." I wanted to kick in a door and race down a hallway, ram someone, anyone, against a wall and grit my teeth into their ear, accuse them of what had happened, because it was their fault, every single stain of wrongfulness making that boy take his life. But before I knew what was happening my hand was back over my shoulder and it was holding the voice-piece that was torn out, the black coiled wire flicking back away from the radio. I dropped it on the seat and left the car parked where it was in the lot.

I was walking and then I was in The Shift and there was a beer in my hand, though I couldn't remember ordering one. It was like a dream that I was walking through, with bits and pieces of the story missing.

Lee Crowley was standing next to me, leaning with his elbow on the bar, watching my face. I wouldn't look at him. I believed that I wanted to tell him a story. I needed to explain, and he understood the need, because he saw what was moving around on my face, having felt it himself, seeing that little girl come in the way she did, knowing the feeling and how it rose to the surface on your skin like a special kind of pain that smelled of a special kind of odour.

I could hear Lee breathing, as if he was getting anxious, or mean, like he believed in something and wanted to fight whatever it was that was troubling me because it was an old enemy that he had faced and lost to.

He said, "Go on." Nodding, he stared down at the bar, convinced this was what he'd been waiting for. "Tell me what happened."

The instant I opened my mouth, the words came out: "You know the area I work? What it's like there. Field Street. You know about Field Street? Everyone knows about it. I ask specifically for that patrol because that part of town needs someone to understand them the most. You have to be at least my size to handle things there. And no one ever knocked me down. Never. No, never. Oh, yeah, except this once. This one time, I was called on a drunk and disorderly. I wasn't far away and I pulled up in the car with my partner. I saw a guy shouting outside his door, but he wasn't shouting to get in like they usually are, pounding the doors to get in late at night and we have to calm them down and try to get them in. This guy was raving at all the houses. So I went up to him and I told him to be quiet. He looked at me and the way he was standing and the shape of his face told me he was crazy, out-of-his-mind drunk. You know? They're the worst of all, like wild animals with a limb torn off. I knew I should've moved back before he had the chance but he was screaming and a flash of his fists hit me. Knocked me down. There was a ringing in my ears when I got up after a few seconds and I knew I heard his door slamming. Boom. I could hear that over the ringing in my ears still in my head. So I just moved forward, fast as I could in the direction of the sound and I aimed with my foot for the place next to the door knob. Something cracked and the door swung open, then stuck, hanging on an angle. The guy was back in the kitchen, shouting and spinning around, knocking things from the shelves and anything in reach. I stayed clear of him, waiting for his body to face me as he scrambled around. He didn't even see that I was there. I waited until he was facing me, then I popped him in the face with my stick. He went down with a lot of noise, and I stepped over him, one boot pinning his shoulder, and I leaned down and kept cracking him in the side of the head, coming down again and again with the back of my fist this time, my hand tight but the skin going softer as I hit him. I popped his ear drum, I found out later, and his old man— who I knew to be a crazy from long ago— got up from his chair in the living room, pushing himself with his cane, and came at me. He was old but he'd have killed me if he could. He was a real bastard. They were the Leonards and they had a wild reputation. So I turned around and waited 'til he got close enough so I could hear his growling and cursing and I slapped the cane out of the air and cracked him in the jaw. He went down sideways, the cane landing across his face when he hit the ground. They were down, but I knew they'd be up in a little while. They were like they were invincible. Anything could happen to them.

"Next day they said they were pressing charges and I was called into the sergeant's office. When he told me, I said, 'Come off it. Leonard hit me first.' And it was soon forgotten. They were just the worst kind of scum."

I glanced up away from my hand and the glass it was holding. Lee wasn't used to hearing me talk this way. He was watching me, waiting and knowing that what I was saying was only the first trembling of words that'd loosen something bigger.

I hadn't tasted my beer yet. I concentrated on the glass and felt that it was still cool but I didn't want a drink. There was this nervous aching in my muscles and bones that made me feel like I didn't want anything.

Lee took a slow sip of his beer. His eyes never left my face. Then he pulled them away and laid down his glass, lining it up with the water ring the bottom of his glass had already made against the bar top.

"Tell me what happened," he said, careful how he sounded.

I turned my head to have a look behind me. People were coming and going. A group toward the back was standing in a circle telling jokes and laughing. The sound of their laughter made me uneasy. There was no need for that kind of disrespect. I wanted to make them stop. That was what I wanted right then.

"Pay no attention to them," Lee said. "They're not laughing at you." The bartender came over and Lee said a few words to him and they both stared at me. The bartender asked Lee a question about my plans for the future. Lee couldn't say one way or the other. I squinted at the bartender and he nodded and moved away to serve a man in a blue raglan with a neat fold of bills in his hand. I took my time studying the bills, then I studied the man's face for a while. I didn't like the looks of him.

"It was a child," Lee insisted. "Wasn't it?" He needed to know. In a strange way it'd mean comfort to him.

"I'm finished," I told him, nodding down at the bar. "Yes. I am. Never again."

"You told me that," he said, but not in a bad way. "Tell me what happened."

"You want to know?"

Lee didn't answer. He just watched my hands, then took a good look at my face like I was one of his patients and he was thinking about what might be done for me.

"Okay, I'll tell you this one." Finally, I took a drink. I needed a drink. The beer was getting warm and the bubbles hurt my throat. I must've made some kind of reaction because Lee called to the bartender, "A cold one." Then he set his attention back on me and said, "I could tell you about the girl again. I swore I never would, but if it helps..."

"No," I said. I had to stop him right away. I couldn't bear another word about that little girl. Not right now. "There was this older lady who used to call down to the station every other weekend. She had two sons: Bobby and Tom. I knew her by name and she always called, asking for me. For me, like I was saying earlier: I understood. The people around there knew me and my tattoos showed in the summer because I'd just wear my short-sleeved shirt and no uniform jacket. The people respected that. They saw that I was marked, so I was in the same ballpark, like one of them. I was mostly a friend down there. People trusted me, but they knew I never took any shit. I understood. Get it? Yeah? Okay, so this woman. Her name was Mrs. Hynes. She'd call down to the station and they'd radio me to go up and help her out. I'd look forward to seeing her because it was no trouble. She was a nice old lady with white hair and a real soft-looking wrinkled-up face. And a great sense of humour. Her sons were bastards. They'd get drunk and fight each other, wreck her house and slap her around. Sometimes she'd be bleeding or bruised and I'd have to take her to the hospital, but it was only for minor cuts or abrasions. She wouldn't complain. She'd tell me it was her flesh who was doing it, and so it was her own fault. She believed this sort of thing. The type who'd put up with anything, from the old school. No disrespect intended. The woman was a saint. So I looked forward to calming down her boys. There's a breaking point for all of us on the force. You know, we're only human beings trying to do our best, so the idea of hurting these boys whenever possible took some of the tension off. It could be justified because they were pricks to start with. It was that simple. No argument. I was fond of Mrs. Hynes. She raised those fuckers with no father and they took control of her, a sweet old woman who didn't deserve the kind of crap she had to put up with. So I get the call that her boys are a little worse than usual. The dispatcher says to make it quick. A different set of codes than before. You know the codes. You know what I'm talking about; the possibility of someone being dead.

I think of Mrs. Hynes and I imagine what I'll do to those two boys if any harm's come to her. I pull up, and the car jolts still when I hit the brakes. I jump out and I'm ready. But I don't forget what I've learned. I knock first, and call out, then I listen with my ear to the door. The place sounds pretty quiet, so I knock again, louder, and Mrs. Hynes opens up. She says, like she's out of breath, 'Brian, I think they've done it this time.' 'Done what?' I ask her. She says, 'I think young Bobby's killed Tom.' 'Okay, relax,' I tell her, 'I'm here now.' I glance into the living room while I'm passing by, heading back to where the kitchen is. It's dark in there but I see Tom leaning against the mantlepiece with his elbow up on the ledge. 'So where's Bobby?' I ask Mrs. Hynes. She tells me he's in the kitchen and I go in there and see he's head-first down on the kitchen table and he's snoring, so everything's okay. Everything's fine. Right?"

I stopped for a second because all the air had gone out of my lungs. I took a deep breath, then watched Lee lift his beer. My face was burning with heat and I was edgy. Someone elbowed me trying to get a place at the bar and I turned my head to give whoever it was the necessary look, and this guy said he was sorry, so I forgave him even though I had trouble with the idea of forgiveness right then. It took me a little while to set my attention back on Lee. I was feeling dizzy, like someone had just pulled me away from being right in the middle of a real situation.

"But there's more to it," Lee said, totally sure of himself. He was almost smiling, a knowing smile that was there to tell me it knew all about lies and tragedy. "Everything's not okay," Lee insisted.

"Is it ever?" I asked him, hearing my voice clear as anything in my ears.

Lee smiled sadly this time and shook his head. He tried to pretend that he was being patient, but his eyes gave him away, the way he kept watching me, encouraging.

"Mrs. Hynes," he said, casually reminding me.

"Yes," I told him, trying not to check out his hands but knowing they were moving around more than usual. "Mrs. Hynes keeps insisting. She won't let up about young Bobby killing Tom. So I tell her, 'I just looked in the living room and he's okay. He's in there leaning up against the mantlepiece. A beer in his hand.' 'No, Brian,' Mrs. Hynes pleads, shaking her old head at me. 'Go in there.' I do as she says, step up into the first room that's got a small dining table I have to move around, and stare into the small box of a living room. I call out Tom's name but he doesn't answer, so I reach for the wall and flick up the switch. Tom's there all right. He's on his feet and he's smiling with his arm back, up on the ledge, and there's a beer bottle in his hand and the bent end of a crowbar pointing out of his chest, the sharp part shoved through him and stuck into the mantlepiece, holding him up."

I licked my lips, tilted my glass and slowly poured in the new beer that the bartender had set down in front of me. Then I lifted the rim to my mouth and quickly drank it because I was thirsty. My lips were really hot. The liquid spilled right past them and they were still hot when I took the last swallow.

"Mrs. Hynes?" Lee asked, scratching the lobe of his ear with his finger. "She reacted how?"

"She spoke really low and watched where her son was dead and I saw that she understood she was going to be alone. In spite of everything, she loved her boys and they cared for her more than anything. You know, it sounds strange, right? But they took care of her. There was more to it than a couple of boys beating on their mother, there's always more to it than that. A strange kind of love mixes everything up. No one could ever understand it."

"Slum love," said Lee. "I know what you mean." He was breathing heavily, drinking faster than I'd ever seen him drink before. The empties were adding up on the bar. He ordered another beer, his eyes sloppy and weak, and the bartender delivered, clearing away the used bottles.

"Painful love that keeps those people together, a whole lot closer because they've all been hurt badly. Years of living hard and with only half a family, so the family gets to be the most important thing. Closer and closer, but still hurting each other because there's no way of ever being complete. Understand? And this was what was keeping *me* from my breaking point. This shaky kind of love. I'd come in and beat those boys and keep it going, keep it going so we could all hang on."

Lee saw the confused look on my face. "I know it," he told me. But he was really feeling the truth of what I was saying and it was making him worse. He just kept watching me, checking my face and eyes and waiting for the details of the story responsible for having us set together like magnets.

"Was it a boy or a girl?" Lee wanted to know. "There's a difference. A difference like you wouldn't believe."

I stared down into my glass and thought I'd never give up another word.

"I swear," I whispered, my shoulders going weak.

"I'll do it for you," Lee said, his voice busting loose as he held up his surgeon hands. I waited for a second before I gave them a look. They were as steady as anything I'd ever seen. Lee coughed real low and swallowed. "The girl was only four years old." And Lee's hands started shaking. He watched them and they got worse. "She came in barely breathing, blood in her lungs, the little sputtering sounds, the hurt crying, weaker and weaker, her small eyes slow and watching me, watching me. No chance..."

I grabbed hold of his arm. I cut him short, and I knew by the way that he stared at my face that he was upset with me for stopping him. He believed that the pain had to be let out, but I didn't think it worked that way. I believed that sort of total release would make him break down. You could come close to it, let off a little steam, but never let the weakness out all at once. It had to be held onto, because a person's pain and weakness was actually the only thing giving them any kind of strength.

"Forget about it," I told him.

Lee put down his trembling hands and finished his beer. Then he turned away without another word and left. I'd said the wrong thing to him. I don't why I did it, but I was feeling lousy for pretending that I didn't really understand.

I finished what was in my glass and had another, then took a taxi back to the house where I'd seen the boy. I stood outside with my hands in my pockets, watching the dark windows and listening to the quiet for a while. The house was your average bungalow, white with black shutters. It had a car in its driveway that hadn't been there the last time and, as I got closer, I noticed how well-kept the grass was on the sloping banks.

I finally made it to the top of the concrete steps. I reached for the doorbell, but froze when I saw light suddenly spilling out on the lawn from the big window. Right away there were clunking noises, too, hurried footsteps against the floor getting louder and closer as someone's hand fumbled around, pulling the doors open from inside.

St. John's, 1990

The Houses of Samuel Taylor

for Edith and Douglas Butler

I

Shortly before his death, Samuel Taylor made an unexpected trip up the rugged coast of Newfoundland. In the first light of dawn, he departed Bareneed in a trap skiff. Incredibly— with the use of only a small engine— he sailed beyond Conception Bay, veering northwest along Fogo, through Norte Dame Bay. He passed Hare Bay, the ragged cut in the tip of the Northern Peninsula, leaving the island behind as he entered the Strait of Belle Isle, an open waterway where the swell of the ocean turned loppy, threatening to capsize his skiff. Unperturbed, Samuel Taylor crossed steadily, heading for Labrador.

Local legend spoke of his heartless suspicion, of how he believed his son and daughter might be after his house in Battle Harbour on the Labrador coast. Arriving there at dusk, he docked at the sagging wharf, his old square house standing alone and without light on the desolate barren. He lifted the tin container of gasoline from his boat and carried it up the slight mossy incline. Stepping willfully, he glanced at the sky, the deepening grey cloud cover muting the deep blue of his eyes. He reached the doorstep and set the container on the grass.

Unlocking the door with a large iron key, he bent for the container, raised it and stepped inside. He thoroughly wiped his boots on the mat, then went about tossing arcing splashes of gasoline here and there, dousing the antique furniture and wallpaper. Convinced of his coverage, his mind wavering from the fumes, he stepped outside, took a deep breath, and glanced around to see what might be lost. Without shift in expression, he struck a wooden match against the patch of flint and tossed it in. The surge of sound and heat made him step back. His jaw remained unclenched while his eyes checked the roof for signs of imminent collapse.

A few Inuit neighbours from along the coast met him as he was leaving with the empty container hanging from one hand. They had docked their boats alongside his and were rushing up in alarm toward the startlingly orange flames and billowing pillar of grey and black smoke. Both men carried white salt meat buckets filled with water sloshing over the sides. They glanced at Samuel as they raced past him on his way to his skiff. Without offering a word or varying his stride, he continued on, climbed on board, pulled the engine cord, and headed out. The open sea at night.

Samuel Taylor had already made certain that no one would occupy his house back in Bareneed, either. He swore he would haunt the place and set a curse on anyone who so much as set foot inside the front door once he had passed off this earth.

Samuel Taylor's wife, Phyllis, sat in her parlour rocking chair, staring at their old house across the Bareneed harbour. The house was set at the base of an enormous headland that rose into the sky, and— at night— became a mass of blackness that was darker than the night itself, a hole cut into the sky with the lights of the few houses set there at its base lit up like miniatures.

Phyllis' son Graham was playing the piano behind her, his slim fingers sweeping over the keys. He briskly turned the yellowed sheet of piano music and smiled at the subsequent curve in tempo, his mouth stirring as if to shape the notes he played passionately.

Phyllis observed a crab boat pulling up to the old tin fish plant; Ira Butler unloading pots from the deck. It was a good distance, but Phyllis' eyesight was still sharp despite her failing health. Graham ended his song, immediately lifting another sheet of piano music that gave the odour of decades past. Head tilted slightly back, he sang along in an exaggerated, delicate tone, the notes lingering. When he was done, he stood and used both sets of fingers to daintily pull the covering over the keys. Thoughtfully, he rubbed the smooth wood with his palm. "I'm going to check on the dough," he informed his mother, who took no notice of him as he left the room.

Phyllis Taylor watched across the water. The old grey house with its grey shop and barn in the shallow back yard that quickly met the dark cliff. How many people had enquired about buying it from her? Graham returned and sat on the low parlour couch beside the piano. Soon, Phyllis heard the clicking of his knitting needles. What was he making now? She turned her head to see that it was a pink infant outfit for his sister, Trina's, baby.

When he saw her looking, he raised the work and grinned. "What'd'ya think, Mommy? Is it lovely?"

"That's fine, Graham," Mrs. Taylor said plainly, then turned to stare back at the house, her wrinkled face set with resignation. She heard her son fuss over something and then rise from the sofa. She heard sounds that she knew could not be present in the house, the whispering trickle of water and then the quickening of its wet rushing. A flood. Staring toward the floorboards, she saw only dry strips of wood. Regardless, the sound became louder, the gushing of a steady brook, the beating of waves against her eardrums, against her skin, her lips, and shut eyelids. The urgent cry of a seagull mounted her brain, the soaring intensity of its vigilant screech deafening.

When Graham rose from where he was bent over his basket, having discovered the ball of pink wool he had been digging for, he turned to pose a question to his mother, but the words remained unspoken. The sight of his mommy slumped forward in her chair jolted him. Gasping, he pressed his fingers against his trembling lips to contain his shriek.

It was a brilliantly sunny day, which braved the mood of the occasion. Trina Taylor stood over her mother's grave and wept openly. She

handed the infant to her husband, Harold, and grasped the handker-
chief offered by him. She wiped at her eyes and nose and wept louder
as she felt Graham's arm rest comfortingly against her shoulders. He
hugged her tightly and she wept even more freely, her mouth
slackened by grief.

"It's okay," Graham said reassuringly, but he spoke the words
through his own confounding sense of loss. He bit his lip and
sniffled, discreetly dabbing at his tears with the cuff of his white
shirt.

The crowd returned to Graham's house for the reception. He accepted
the condolences and the equally welcome compliments regarding the
fine table he had laid out. Ham and turkey and various sorts of cold
salads he'd made himself, up all night baking, keeping busy. Cookies,
cakes and pies, the sweets sent over from the neighbours.

Glancing around the room, Graham suffered the keen perception
often paired with sleeplessness. The people in the kitchen were all so
peculiar and yet so wonderful in their specific mannerisms. He was at
odds with his emotions as he watched them eating. They were so
blessed to be here, he told himself, on this earth. All such good people,
yet he felt animosity towards them for simply being alive. He moved
down the hallway toward the parlour and— sighting his sister sitting
with her infant— joined her on the couch.

"How you doing, Sis?" He laid his hand on her knee, awaiting
her reply.

She shrugged and swallowed hard, her eyes rimmed pink, the
blackness of her dress making her fair skin seem ghostly, her orange
hair vibrant. "I have to feed Joshua," she said, rising without considering either of the people who glanced compassionately at her,
wondering of her movements. Graham followed her upstairs, into their
mother's room, where Trina sat on the edge of the bed and lowered
the front of her dress.

"I know about your troubles," Graham said outright, watching the baby instinctually search for and then clamp onto the nipple.

"Everyone must have heard," Trina said morosely.

"No, no. From mother. No one else knows." He patted her head. "Don't you think that, Trinny."

They both were silent, only the hungry sounds of the infant snorting, sucking, swallowing.

"You have to live here," Graham said. "There's no question. I won't hear another word." He covered his ears and turned away dramatically, about to leave the room. "I'll disown you if you don't." He began humming and carried on with the sound for a few moments. When he lowered his hands, he heard her say: "He's done, I think."

Graham faced Trina and anxiously took the infant while his sister did up her dress. "Come to Uncle Graham, little Joshua."

"Harold says the bank'll take our house in a few weeks. We can't keep up the payments." Trina stared worriedly at Graham, a deadness in her eyes, while her brother rocked the infant on his shoulder. "These layoffs. They're murder."

"Shush, shh-shh-shh."

"He really settles with you," she said flatly, nodding. She held a crumpled tissue in both her hands, moving it back and forth, lightly picking at it. She glanced at the open doorway, aware of the sounds of the crowd downstairs.

"And what will Harold think of this? Us, all together in one happy little home? It'll take the strain off, you think?"

Trina sighed and surveyed the cream-coloured dresser, the photograph of her mother and father in their wedding clothes, a photograph that their mother had put up following their father's death. Samuel had forbidden the displaying of photographs.

"If only Harold hadn't lost his job."

"Not another word. I'm warning you. This is your home, Trinny. This is little Joshua's home."

Trina gave him a quiet smile and observed him rocking the baby.

"You just let me know when you want to move in and I'll clear the space for you." He tilted his head down to kiss Joshua on the top of his soft head. "He's just so gorgeous, such a little miracle."

II

Harold sat watching Graham crocheting a powder blue doily for the church soiree.

"Cabin fever yet?" Graham asked, darting a polite glance at Harold.

"No." He stood and switched on the television. "Not at all."

"A long way from the city. What do you like to do?"

"It's not that far," he said, eyes fixed on the television screen as he sat again.

"Not much work around here; even the fishing's dried up. There's no end to it. What a shame, you think?"

Harold nodded. He watched the television for a few more moments— feigning interest in a popular talk show— then shifted his eyes to glance briefly at Graham.

Graham heard them arguing from his mother's bedroom. It was twenty past eleven by the white wind-up clock ticking at the side of his bed. He rolled toward the window, hearing the baby crying. A tugging in his heart. He stirred, wishing to rise and fetch the infant. The voices grew louder as his mother's door was opened. Harold's voice, "You just think about Joshua."

Then the baby's cries died out as he was comforted by his mother.

"He would never do anything," Trina said in a controlled whisper, then shushed the infant back to sleep.

Graham imagined her standing there in his sewing room, all

cleared-out for the baby. His sewing machine and chair moved to the corner of his bedroom. The door to his mother's room shut as Harold returned.

Graham listened to his sister's sweet voice, singing: "Silent Night, Holy night, all is calm, all is bright. Round yon Virgin, Mother and child..." just as their mother had done to them. Sighing, he shut his moist eyes, and was beginning to drift off when he heard the muffled sounds of arguing voices recommence.

Once again, he came wide awake, thinking on the chores for the morning. He could not sleep and so rose and tiptoed out into the hallway. Passing the sewing room, at the head of the stairs, he leaned in to assure himself the infant was sleeping soundly. His greatest fear was that Joshua might stop breathing, and he could not bear the thought of that. A dead little baby. He shuddered at the idea and crept further into the room to discover Joshua asleep on his back.

Graham stared at the small chest, trying to detect the rising and falling by the vague starlight beyond the narrow window. He reached in and warily felt the baby's neck. It was warm. Satisfied, he turned.

"Eeeee!" he shrieked. A man was lurking there, so near. At first, Graham feared it might be the ghost of his father, Samuel. Why he thought of his father, he had no idea.

"What're you doing in here?" the voice demanded.

"God help me!" Graham cried out.

The light was switched on, assaulting his eyes. He squinted to see that it was Harold standing in the doorway.

"Oh." Graham pressed a hand to his chest and swallowed hard. "Harold, it's you. I... I was checking on Joshua." He turned, relieved, reached into the crib to straighten the blankets, but his hand was roughly snatched and yanked back. He was shoved aside by Harold in a way that left Graham stunned, jaw agape, tears bulging in his eyes.

"You're not allowed in here," Harold said, his tone tempered, not nearly as threatening, but his breath heavy in his nostrils. He stared at

Graham's expression, the terrible hurt, the hand darting to his trembling lips. Harold strode away, out of the room, leaving the light on. Graham hurried toward the doorway, switching off the light on his way out. He scampered downstairs to the parlour and sat at the piano. He searched out the sheet music for "Amazing Grace" and began playing quietly. Drawing in a deep breath, he shut his eyes and sang from the very bottom of his heart, to calm himself.

"No," Graham assured Trina. "No, no, no. *You* stay. You're a *family*." He smiled brightly, reassuringly. "It's okay. There's the other house across the water."

Trina's eyes widened a touch. "Father's house."

"That's nonsense." Graham tore the risen dough into bun-sized blobs and set them in the greased bread pan. "You're a family. You need your privacy. I understand completely. I understand, Trinny. Don't worry."

"Then let Harold fix the roof."

Graham stopped what he was doing to turn and consider her; he determined that this gesture would mean a great deal to his sister, and so he nodded, "Okay. That'd be fine."

"Okay." She smiled, for the first time in days. "Great." Leaning close, she kissed Graham on the cheek.

"But I'll buy the shingles," he said firmly. "Harold's labour is more than enough of a gift."

Graham sat in his mother's chair, rocking Joshua. He watched across the water, seeing the dot on the roof of his father's house and the dot on the ground that he knew was Lloyd Hawco, a brawny young fellow from the community who Harold had hired to gum the shingles and hoist up to the roof.

Trina was watching a soap opera and eating a box of caramel popcorn.

"Who's Alexis seeing now?" Graham asked.

"Trent."

"She's a real slut, you think?" He glanced at Trina, then sucked in his breath, clamped his lips tight. "Sorry," he said, mortified, eyeing the infant.

"I don't think Joshua can understand yet."

Relieved, Graham faced the window again. He saw the late afternoon light stretching across the dark blue water and then he saw Harold descending from the roof, carefully moving down the tall wooden ladder. "He's coming home," Graham said, rising from his rocker and swiftly handing the infant to his sister. "I better check supper," he announced, and dashed from the room.

III

Graham hadn't been in the house for over fifteen years. The thought of entering it again had always terrified him. He found that the door was unlocked when he gripped and turned the cold knob.

Lingering in the open doorway, captivated by the rush of memories, he glanced back across the harbour toward the house they had lived in after his father's death, the house that his father had bought from a destitute sinner of the Church of England, the house Graham had lived in for most of his life, now occupied by his sister and her family.

He stepped into his childhood home and was struck by the damp odour of mildew and rot. The furniture and portraits remained in their exact places. No one had dared break into the abandoned house to destroy or steal the objects once belonging to Samuel Taylor. Not even one window had been smashed.

The place would require a great deal of work before he could move his things over. The wallpaper was peeling at the corners. He would have to strip it and paint the walls or have gyprock erected. A new chimney for the fire, to drive the damp out. He would have to hire someone to accomplish most of this. He would use the money he had put away for just such an emergency. He was glad he had not offered it to Trina. It would only have been spent on a bad mortgage. Gone. This way, Trina, Harold, and little Joshua had a house that no one could take away from them.

Graham set his foot on the first stair. After pausing a moment, he continued up, hearing the subsequent stairs creaking beneath his feet until he reached the top and turned to see his parents' bedroom. The elegance of the room, despite the years it had endured, softened his heart. He was struck with sentimental longing as he ventured down to his and his sister's old bedroom. Their beds were set in the exact positions he remembered. The crucifixes above each of the beds. The faded blue painting of the Virgin Mary over the dresser, half covered by a fallen sheet of wallpaper.

Everything was in its place. Nothing was to be removed after Samuel's death. It had been stipulated in his will. Nothing was to be removed. Everything was to be bought new for their new lives without him. Toys could not be taken away. Even their clothes were to be left to rot in the closets. Samuel Taylor had hoarded enough money to ensure the purchase of new goods. Nothing was to leave the house and no one was to enter it again. No one was to disturb the objects of the past life of Samuel Taylor.

Graham sat on his bed, marvelling at the sights around him, his childhood preserved exactly as it had been at the time of his father's death. He stood— unwilling to touch a single item— and wandered into his mother's room to stop before the dust-covered artifacts on her dresser, her silver comb and brush set, her bevelled glass perfume bottle with its black atomizer, the long strings on its tassel, her blue glass rosary beads with the attached medals of saints. He wanted so desperately to touch, but he refrained from doing so. His mother's closet door was open and he stared at her clothes, shuddered at the memories of how they had once been worn. He held his arms. It was so chilly. He felt a sneeze coming on, the distress of it intensifying and then expelling itself. He was dismayed by the loudness of the sound and the particles of dust that had been disturbed into the light.

Back in his bedroom, he sat on his bed. What was he to do now? His carved wooden boat rested on the floor and— giving in to the temptation— he reached for it. Studying the design, his heart sank through those years. Childhood. He lay back on his bed. How could one not find such exquisite melancholic joy there? He ran his slim fingertips over the boat's grooves. His father Samuel had carved it and handed it to him without instruction or expectation. A stern plain man, Graham told himself while examining the boat.

"Amazing," he whispered, hearing a creaking of the floorboards slightly beyond the bedroom doorway. He shot up in his bed and leapt to his feet, remaining still, listening alertly.

"Graham," a low voice called out to him, the frail voice of a visitor entering from below, the voice so much resembling his mother's.

"Yes," he blurted out, uncertain of who had spoken.

"Your father wants to know what you're doing here."

The boat dropped from Graham's fingers, a tingle rising in the hairs on his arms and neck and then travelling throughout his skin. He crept to the door and leaned out, expecting the head of his father to rear and face him. Peeking out further, he whimpered when he saw the empty hallway. His skin was tight with gooseflesh. His heart was punishing him. He was sweating profusely.

Without thinking, he hurriedly tiptoed down the stairs, gaining speed before running for the open front door, grunting, almost yelping. He scampered down to the lower road until halted by the edge of the water. Eyes jammed shut, hands squeezed into fists in front of his chest, he remained rigid, as if the bony fingers of some apparition might clasp his shoulder at any moment.

He waited, hardly drawing breath. When he thought he might be safe, he turned, cringing in the dusk to regard the house. He saw the opened door he had— moments ago— fled through. A gaping invitation.

He glanced toward his old bedroom window and saw a boy standing there in the darkness, a girl coming up behind him to watch out over the water, their faces familiar yet indistinct.

And Graham remembered standing in that exact position, staring out over the ocean to capture the return of his father, until— one evening— Samuel Taylor did not find his way back to the wharf. Not a single trace discovered of him in the subsequent years, despite the claims and assurances of most people in the community that something would have to wash up eventually, somewhere on the hard desolate shores of the island.

Graham would not return to the house his sister now occupied. He was in too much of a state. And he certainly would not reenter his childhood home.

As night grew blacker around him, he wandered the community, until it was utterly, unforgivingly dark and chilly to the bone. He paused at the white fence that framed his Aunt Barb's yard. The light in the front room was on and so he ventured up the slate path, around to the back door and opened it.

The air in the kitchen was warm and specific to his aunt. The radio was playing a song he remembered from quite some time ago, a scratchy tune featuring piano and horn. Graham called out to his aunt, but no reply came in return. He found her in the parlour, sitting in her rocking chair, a yellow crocheted blanket over her lap, entranced by the fire in the woodstove. She turned her head to regard him.

"Graham," she said in her brittle old woman's voice. "I thought I heard someone. How're you doing, my love?"

"Fine." He sat across from her, catching his breath, wiping the fresh sweat from his brow.

"Were you walking?"

"Yes, around the harbour." He puffed out a breath and slapped his hands down on his thighs. "A brisk walk. Healthy." He smiled nervously. "Must lose a few pounds, you think?"

She watched him evenly. "Will you have a cup of tea?"

"No, thanks." He rubbed his hands together, banishing the chill of outdoors.

"I saw you over across the harbour." She peered toward her front window that faced the water. "You went in, didn't you?"

"Well, I..." He stopped himself in the proposition of a lie, nodded instead.

Aunt Barb smiled. "Samuel forbade that. And you know what he's like. My brother was a man of his word." She raised a quavering wrinkled hand, positioning it before her face, held it mightily, then let it drop.

"I was going to live there," Graham announced. "Am going to."

"No." She languidly shook her head, "no, no, no..." and stared at him with wet humour in her eyes. "I see Trina and her lot are living in your mother's place."

"Yes."

"That Harold fella."

"What?"

"Townies don't know anything. They're a lazy stupid bunch."

Graham said, "He fixed the roof," and pointed toward the window.

"You stay here, my love, with me. Your father told me that I'd be the one to look after you."

"When? When was that? You never—"

"Years ago."

"Really?" Graham glanced around the room. He saw the old rosebud wallpaper and the piano that he loved, and his nerves began to settle.

"You have such lovely fingers," said his aunt. "Will you play me a tune?"

"I don't know if I can."

"You do play so nicely." She proudly raised her chin, then laboured to stand. On her feet, she noiselessly stepped toward the window to stare at the night. "You were over at the old place," she said. "What was it like?"

"Exactly as we left it."

"No!" She sucked in breath, pivotted to look at him; a quick lithe action, that of a much younger woman. "I too once went over there. Did you know that, Graham? I never told you?"

Graham shook his head. A log crackled loudly in the woodstove. Graham flinched, his eyes darting toward it. He felt the mood shift, his Aunt's eyes brighten.

"You know it was the home of us as children. When me and your father and your Uncle Thomas and Uncle Stephen were children. You knew that."

Graham nodded and licked his lips. His mouth was dry, unbecoming.

"They're all gone now." She patiently returned her gaze to the window. "I went over there after Samuel died, a few months after, and it was the same as when *I* was a child. The exact, like you say, only it was *my* childhood." She regarded him and Graham felt the tingling of gooseflesh rising on his arms. "Samuel was a strict man. He burnt his house up on the Labrador. Everyone knows that story."

"Yes. Why'd he do that?" Graham shifted in his seat. His breathing became heavier. He was growing agitated again. He shook his head in a troubled manner and crossed his legs, then uncrossed them.

"He knew he was dying," his aunt said patiently. "He just wanted to hold onto his life."

"I heard that he didn't want anyone to have—"

"That story is a wasp's nest of lies, Graham. You probably heard he burned it down because he didn't want you and Trina to have it. That's just foolish people talking. He wanted you and Trina and your mother to start new. So you wouldn't have to live with the memories of him everywhere."

Graham stared at the floorboards, his expression strained.

"You didn't believe that story?" Aunt Barb leaned forward. "Graham, you didn't think he was spiteful like that, did you?"

Graham slowly shook his head. "I was so young when he—"

"When I was over there," Aunt Barb explained, "it was exactly as we left it when we were children, when my father died and he forbade our return to the house. We lived in *this* house after our father's death. But Samuel never took heed and went back to occupy the house when he wed your mother, to disturb what was meant to be left resting, and your father's life was one of misery. It was a confused life, so closely attached as it was to others."

Standing, Graham felt dizzy. He wiped his sweaty palms on the front of his trousers, uncertain of why he had risen to his feet.

"You stay here with me," Aunt Barb said, smiling and contentedly returning to her rocking chair. Sitting with a groan, she tugged the crocheted blanket up over her lap. "This is your house, now." She gestured with an open hand toward the piano. "You play so well. Would you?"

Graham stared at the piano. Honouring the invitation, he drifted over and clumsily sat at the stool, glad to be off his feet again. He raised the rounded covering and set his fingers against the keys without pressing hard enough to engage a sound. He drew a deep, shivering breath.

"I remember when you used to play as a child," his aunt reminisced. "You had a natural gift. I remember how everyone sat around and watched you. Everyone was there. Do you remember? Everyone came to see you. We were all there. 'Play a song for us, Graham,' we used to say. Everyone looked forward to it on a Sunday, after the big cook-up. It was the only time I ever saw your father smile, standing behind you when you played, watching and listening. The only time."

The image of his father smiling stabbed at Graham's heart. He pictured his father's stern face, the ominous bulk of him. Bracing this unwelcome memory, Graham hesitantly began to play, the bones in his hands aching gracelessly. He paused, bent his fingers, shut his eyes and then opened his palms, straightened, stretching the muscles connecting his fingers. He recommenced.

Soon, his shoulders were moving to the inspirational percussions of the music.

"Sing the words," his aunt called out, her chair rocking evenly, creaking. "Sing them so your father can hear across the harbour."

Graham began to sing, his voice filled with generous high-pitched splendour, joyous tears in his eyes flooding his view of the notes.

"Such a sweet gentle voice," his aunt whispered, beneath the music, "such a sweet gentle boy."

Burnt Head, 1997

The Flesh So Close

My mother has been missing for three days, but I have certain understandings with regards to her whereabouts. There is no need to panic. I look for her in a narrow row house on Maxie Street where Kig is holding an axe in his hands when I come in the door. He is standing at the top of the stairs, and he shows me a kind smile and the space where his front tooth has been knocked away. He watches me with small eyes set so close they seem crossed. Blinking, his bottom lip rises, and his face looms larger, blanker, with the closing of those eyes. His hair— as usual— is greasy, standing up in back and sparsely plastered to his forehead. Kig is not wearing a shirt. The skin along his stomach is white and loose. His arms are the same.

"Mom not here," he calls down in his flat voice. The stairway is windowless and holds the musty smell of rotting wood. I turn back and open the front door a little wider so that light slants in across the blackened floor, then up the first three steps.

"I know she's here, Kig," I tell him, gripping the wobbly rail, feeling it draw toward me as I climb. "She has to come home."

"No." He shakes his head from one side to the other, sharply, as if cutting a thought in half. His eyes keep watching me. Then they shut and remain closed for a moment. When they open again, he says, "No, she stay here, Henry. She stay here. She with me and Carol and Wall."

I take the steps one at a time until I reach the top. I move in front of Kig without giving him the slightest stain of attention. He holds the axe and stares, medicated eyes shifting as I pass. I know he makes no effort to move because I do not hear his footsteps following me as I step through the open apartment doorway.

The first thing I notice is Carol standing by the plastic-sheeted window, a pacifier twitching in her mouth. She is staring at the ground and I wave at her— even though she does not see me— before turning my attention toward the bedroom door. I wait to hear the shuffle of Kig's footsteps coming from behind. He has wandered into the room, cradling the axe, but forgetting about it, more interested in what is going to happen, numbly aware of how he has no power at all.

I reach for the knob on the bedroom door. Mom watches me appear on the threshold. She is lying on the bed, beneath an off-white sheet and an orange tattered quilt that has been kicked down toward the foot of the mattress. A man has his hairy arm around her and I know by his snoring that it is Wall.

"Henry," says my mother, but her face doesn't change. "Henry," she blurts out, the sound like a hiccup.

"I was worried."

"Okay, Henry." My mother stays where she is, her hands beneath the sheets. Her hair is curly and brown and looks as if it was cut lopsided, probably by Wall when he was drunk.

My mother watches me, her face as soft as it can go, and I understand how she would touch me if she could, lay her slow fingers against my skin and rub forcefully, lovingly, until she had smeared her laughing devotion into me. I do not say another word. Mom feels the silence. Her smile is nervous: all lips and gums before it fades away, forgetting what it was there for.

"Don't want go home, Henry."

Kig shuffles close to my side so he can tilt his head to get a better view of my face. He stares; he's forgotten who I am. His thick brows knit and he holds the axe out to me. He shakes his head and pulls back the axe. Remembering.

"What you doing here, Henry?" he asks.

"I'm just making sure Mom is okay."

"Mom fine, Henry. She staying here. She, Wall. Wall sleeping. And Carol out there." He points with the axe blade, toward the open bedroom door.

I focus on the outer room. Carol is standing by the window, eyes fixed on the floor. One pale finger rises and hooks in the pink plastic ring of her pacifier, her arm hanging there. When I look back at Kig, I see that he is nodding as if coaxing me, and I remember when we were children; I have many memories of playing, but for Kig those memories were yesterday or this morning with no distance from point to point. Childhood opens and concludes the impish range of Kig's existence.

"Mom okay, Henry. Look." He tilts the heavy blade toward my mother and she offers the gum-sheening smile. In seconds, it melts away, her doughy eyes wounded. She tries to smile again, more quietly. Withdrawn.

"Staying with Wall, Henry."

"I just wanted to see you were okay, Mom." I step near to her side of the bed. Movement outside the curtainless window draws my attention. It is easy to glance up and see the rooftops across the street. They are flat and run in a line along Slattery. Three houses down, two children stand toward the edge of a roof, their bodies sharply outlined against the white sky. They hold hands and spin in circles, swirling until they lose their grip and fly away from each other. Giddily, they collapse close to an eave on the tar-paper sheeting. They must brace their palms against the roof, their heads taking control, mixing everything up. It is the funniest thing they know, this frightening unbalanced humour of youth promptly lifting them to their feet where they stagger, stop, and squat down. The sense of disparity makes them laugh uncontrollably. They must hold onto their bellies to contain themselves, growing weaker and weaker. It becomes a struggle to stand. They teeter on their feet, then race for each other, hug foolishly, lock fingers and swirl with the spinning force of their union wanting to fling them apart. Heads thrown back, hair reaching away, they know when to release. Their arms fly up into the air, their tiny feet running backwards to catch balance.

I face the room to see Kig waiting by the metal dresser. It was a wedding gift from the institution. Long before I was born, the workers gave it to Wall. Wall has told me: "It was old and they were going to throw it out anyway. Don't think they did something for me. People giving you their garbage. Feeling like saints for doing it."

Kig leans the axe handle against the side of the dresser. He uses all of his fingers, takes his time, ensuring the wooden handle will not slip against the steel. Then he steps back— still bent over— watching it, making certain it is not going to move.

Wall's snoring stutters. He gags and grumbles. His leg kicks beneath the sheet and he coughs a roar. My mother's eyes shift to look at him, knowing he is going to wake. Kig watches, too. He watches the axe, then he watches Wall. Next thing, he holds out his fingers and stares at them, wiping them against his bare chest.

"Wall waking now," Kig says to his hands. "Didn't touch."

And Wall rolls over, his round sleep-etched face rising as he pushes up on one palm. Leaning on his elbows, he squints with true bitterness and surveys the room, studies me and Kig and wonders what the hell is so interesting in his bedroom.

"What'd'ya want?" he snaps at me, falling back onto the bed and moaning, coughing violently, speaking between the punch of each cough: "What's the... problem, Henry. Jesus... Christ! I have to... see you here."

"I think it's time Mom came home and got cleaned up."

Wall lifts his head and stares accusingly at Kig.

"Didn't I tell you to keep him out?" His face goes red, the rage charging through him. He shouts, "The axe. What'd I say to you about that? Use it."

Kig's shoulders slouch, his neck appearing longer and thicker. He moves his hands away from where they were dangling at his sides and rubs the front of his thighs. Tears sheen in his eyes. Crying an open-mouthed sob, he stops right away, wiping at his face with his wrists.

Wall throws his good leg over the edge of the bed, then points at the flesh-coloured plastic leg leaning in the corner. His finger keeps pointing, jabbing the air, until Kig moves for the leg, uses both hands to pass it to Wall. Wall snatches it away. He straps it on, buckles it, and hoists himself up, swinging his leg into action.

"Get the fuck out of my apartment. This is my apartment and I'm taking care of your brother already, your sister. I don't need you, too. I don't need to take care of you again. You get it, Henry. I raised you up. Don't forget it." He is standing close and I can smell the foulness of his breath, the beat of his threatening words; moist and dry at once. "I'll take care of you if you want me to. You know, the way I take care of you won't be nothing special." His lips jitter with the notion and he licks at the gratifying smile overtaking him.

"I have to get Mom home and wash her clothes. A bath to—"

"She's clean," Wall interrupts, giving me a shove and brushing past. "She's got no clothes to worry about," striding and swinging his plastic leg, kicking at a shoe, swinging at whatever's in his way on the floor.

"I'll let you get dressed," I tell my mother, noticing her purple sweat pants and shirt in a clump by the side of the bed. "Okay?"

"No," she says, staying right where she is, not having stirred an inch since I came into the room. Her eyes blink thoughtlessly and I wonder about the mascara and eye shadow blotched along the tops of her cheeks. I remember how Wall used to do her up when I was a child. He insisted she was entitled to this one touch of female extravagance. ("Make her a real woman," he always claimed.) But I came to understand that he took great pleasure in dragging the make-up haphazardly across her face when he was loaded. He enjoyed trying to change her body, moving her naked limbs in extreme directions, wondering how far she could bend. He'd stumble back from what he had done to get a better look, the expression on his face disclosing everything: he was hoping my mother's body would stay fixed in the pose he had arranged.

Kig sits on the edge of the bed, close to my mother, and sloppily strokes her curly hair. He uses the flat of his palm and presses down, swiping, distracted.

"Mom," he says, but he is watching me. "Mom."

"Let Mom get dressed, Kig," I tell him. But he stays there, staring at me, squinting resentfully, as if trying to discover who I really am, what all of this could possibly mean to me.

"You. Go now. Go, Henry." He flicks his hand in the air and shakes his head, jerking it from side to side. "Go."

"Go," says my mother, and her chubby pink-skinned arm shoots up from under the sheet. She mimics Kig, pointing with a stiff finger. "You," she says.

"Go," they say.

The frustration makes me turn from the bedroom. I do not glance back. Instead, I reach behind for the knob and draw the door shut. Stepping away, I hear Kig crying. I hear my mother crying. I know they are fearfully clutching onto each other, shivering at the thought of how they will be wrestled apart.

Wall stands in front of the opened refrigerator. I stare at his leg and the light from the fridge gleaming off the dull pink plastic. The counter is littered with beer cans and rum bottles with cigarette butts turned soggy at the damp bottoms. The cupboards are doorless. A few stray tins occupy the shelves. My attention moves from the rusted rim of the stainless steel sink back to Wall's leg. I count the notches in the leather strap that helps hold the leg in place. A piece of his faded green boxer shorts is pinched between his stump and the leg, and I want to move over and tug it free, but I know this would incite a confrontation, so I ignore the nervous twinges urging me to rectify this imperfection.

Wall turns his neck to look back at Carol. The plastic sheeting on the window sucks in, then rounds out, despite the absence of wind. Carol stares at me. The pacifier jerks in her mouth as her jaw shifts, sucking. Her white arms are short and hang above her hips. Her stumpy fingers straighten, slowly bend, then straighten again and remain rigid as if a shrill sound has been cracked from a shell. Her soiled nightdress is frayed along the hemline and ripped straight down below her belly. Her body presses beneath the cotton see-through material, the sides of her trapped breasts spilling at the torn arm holes.

Wall passes no comment. He turns his attention back toward the fridge, staring in but seeing nothing, planning instead. I look to sit on the couch, but discover that the couch is gone, so I remain standing, bending one knee to take the weight off my lower back.

"What happened to your couch?" I ask, trying to ease the tension.

"Nothing," Wall barks, staring into the ice box. I know his thoughts are tightening, each word from me poisoning the situation. No doubt he interprets the mere sound of my voice as conspicuous provocation. He is mad, and planning what to do with me, wondering what can be pulled from the shelves of the fridge and hurled my way. It is not a new game. I have yet to face a single surprise here; Wall's violence is as predictable as the direction drawn by gravity. I watch him, waiting to duck or lean from the path of flying objects.

"It's gone," I tell him.

"What does that prove? Shut up."

"I don't know what it proves."

Glancing over his shoulder, his eyes are dark slits. He has not shaved for days. Prickly grey and white stubble grows along his jaw and high on his cheeks. The stubble matches the colour of his hair. It is clipped short, an oval-shaped bruise visible along his scalp.

"I don't like doing this every time," I must tell him. "I've got custody." I emphasize the last word because I need for him to understand the importance of it. "You can't hurt Mom any more. You might've got custody of Carol and Kig, but I got Mom away from you."

Wall's face swells red. He growls: "Away from no one. I can tell you as your father, no, that doesn't mean shit to you, so I'll tell you as someone who might just punch the fuck out of you." He slams the refrigerator door, things rattling loose inside, and spins around, teetering. "Man to man, if that's what you like. None of this law crap. The way you always like fighting me. You get no one away from no one. Ever. The law's not human. It's a fucking joke."

"I'm only looking after her like the courts told me to do."

"Because I can't," he shouts, kicking back with his plastic leg, driving a dent in the refrigerator, then limping forward, closer, glaring at me. "Right?" His face has darkened to a beet red, and he curses with thick white saliva in the corners of his mouth. "Because you're better."

I shake my head.

"Because I've hit her once or twice to teach her a thing." His eyes round from his face. He stops to swallow, to catch a quick breath. "Not to touch, not to touch this or that." The tendons in his throat pull to get away from him. Even his ears have gone red. "Not to piss on the floor like she used to when I first met her. She doesn't do that any more because I showed her she couldn't. Let's go way back to when I was working in the fucking nut house, cleaning up the floors that she was pissing on. When I met her and she was locked in a cage. Let's go back there. A nice-looking young woman locked away. You remember where I took her from." He swipes the saliva from his mouth with the back of his hand, then uses his palm to do his chin. "You're too stupid to keep that in mind."

"I've heard it all, Wall."

"Heard it all. Heard nothing," he threatens, limping one step closer. "How they strapped her to a bed and tied her down when she fucked up in the slightest." He holds up one hand, grabbing at something in the air. He squeezes his fingers into a fist and his lips turn white and hard. "I showed her what it was like to be with a man. And that's it. That's what she wanted, to be complete like that. Then she showed some manners and was like she belonged. I put something in her that she never had and I took her out of there. I looked after her long before there was you, you little shit-stain fucker."

I step away from him, but keep him in the corner of my eyes. Some concern must be directed toward Carol because she is shivering now. I put my arm around her shoulders and tenderly draw her close. The trembling increases. She quietly shrieks in her throat. I rub her arm and try to check her eyes. But they shift away from me as she sucks and chews on her pacifier.

Wall wants to say more. He limps another step toward me, but suddenly lurches to a stop, interrupted by the misplacement of open space. "Hey," his voice is surprisingly shrill, "where's the couch?" He darts a glance at me as if I have it stuffed up under my shirt.

"That's what I was asking earlier," I blankly tell him.

"Fucking Christ!" He limps over to the apartment door and throws it open, sticks his head out, leaning to get a good look up the hall. He shouts a threat at someone who isn't there, some thief who has already escaped. Limping back in, he uses both hands to slam the door.

"The couch," he accuses, kicking the wall with his plastic toes. The toes sink in, get stuck deep in the hole he's made. Wall struggles to pull them free, but then loses his balance, tumbles sideways onto the floor.

"Get away from me," he says, pulling his arm loose when I bend to help him. "You're nothing to me, you know-it-all freak." He yanks the toes from the hole and rolls over on his belly, pushing himself up. On his feet, he kicks the heel of his plastic leg against the floor to straighten the hinge at the knee. "You're nothing to me, Henry. I don't know why the hell I kept you around for so long. I should've drowned you in the toilet for being so fucking perfect. Trouble. Thinking you were better. Always saying things to the others. Correcting them. Teaching them useless crap they'd never understand. You do something, you teach them the rules. That's all they need to know. The rules to get by. That's everything. They get by. You remember that. Kig's my only real son now. Carol over there's my daughter, and Doreen's my wife. She's your mother, yes, okay. But I won't claim to be your father any more. I know why you don't need me. Because you're crazy, that's why." He storms around the apartment, searching for a place to stop, but he keeps limping, circling, questioning the floor. "I don't know where you came from."

"I know all that, Wall." I stare at the bedroom door. The crying has stopped and I understand that Mom and Kig are just holding each other now, eyes wide open and glaring into the flesh so close to them, not close enough, and wondering, expecting the worst.

Wall stops, then swings his leg over near to me, studies my eyes.

"You're crazy," he says, nodding once, solidly, to confirm this indisputable fact. "You think you're the best, that's why. You're the worst thing I've ever seen."

I watch him, inspecting the disbelief in his face, wait for more.

"You think things are so simple. Black and white." He draws back his fist and swings for the side of my chin, but I dodge him and he skips to keep balance, topples. When his body pounds the floor, I hear a quiet gasp from Carol. I look over and her fingers are straight, her jaw working frantically, shifting the nipple around in her mouth as if struggling to escape. She stares at me, not even noticing Wall, only feeling the sound of how his body has struck the floor, sensing the violating rumble against the bottoms of her bare feet.

Wall stays down and spins in circles, cursing and kicking, spinning around and around, his jaws slashing like a mad dog's.

"You... ahrrr... worst," he sputters, "the worst... hhhhorrible..."

I edge away from him, move for the bedroom door. It opens easily and I step in to face stillness and quiet. At first, I think Kig and my mother are gone. For an instant it seems as if they have disappeared, but then— as I step closer— I notice the two lumps under the twisted bed sheets.

The noise behind me has subsided. Wall has spun himself out, uncoiled all of his cursing and agitation. I glance back to see him lying on the floor, mutely staring at the ceiling. His chest rises and settles with calming breaths. "Doreen?" he quietly mutters. His throat moves as he swallows. He wipes at his eyes, whispering: "Kig? Carol?"

I step toward the iron bed. Two bodies beneath the sheets, secretively attempting to hold onto the air they must draw. The covers stir as one of them carefully shifts. The cautious sound of contained whimpering.

"Come on, now," I say. My fingers ache with impatience; they reach down and whisk back the sheet.

I see what I expect: my mother and Kig, naked and desperately hugging. Kig's flesh is loose and white, my mother's loose and pink. Their eyes are scrunched shut, jamming tighter when they feel the cool untroubled air coaxing them to press nearer.

I ask no questions.

My mind has learned to accept what it sees, insisting that I have never been startled by the images facing me, nor by the actions that can follow. I am rarely touched by emotions, but I sense things all the same: a cool damp hand against the back of my neck. The weak grip that I recognize as Carol's. And I am right. I am correct. She is standing there when I turn, her stubby fingers jabbing, forcing the pacifier between my lips.

St. John's, 1991

ACKNOWLEDGEMENTS

PREVIOUSLY PUBLISHED
"Above the Movements of Night" first published in *Canadian Author,* Spring, 1995
"Arrow and Heart Tattoo" first published in *NeWest Review*, June/July, 1992
"Behind Glass" first published in *Event*, Summer, 1989, and anthologized in *Hard Times* (Aya/Mercury), 1990
"Better Not Mind Nothing" first published in *Venue*, December 1994
"The Broken Earth" first published in *Quarry* and *Oberon's Best Canadian Stories*, 1995
"A Coward" first published in *Exile*, Volume 21, Number 3, 1998
"Fitting Circles into Squares" first published in Event, Volume 27, Number 2, 1998
"The Flesh So Close" first published in *Books in Canada*, March, 1992
"The Houses of Samuel Taylor" first published in *TickleAce*, Number 35, Summer, 1998.
"Idling Car As Seen Through Fog" first published in *The Fiddlehead,* Summer, 1997
"Lightning Dust" first published in *Matrix*, Fall, 1993
"Love Story For Jan" first published in *Venue,* Summer, 1996
"Merciful Hope" first published in *The Fiddlehead*, and *Panurge* (England), October, 1992
"Muscle" first published in *TickleAce*, Volume 29, Spring/Summer 1995
"A Natural Thing" first published in *Exile,* Volume 13, Number 2, 1994
"The Plastic Superman" first published in *The Canadian Forum* November, 1994, and *Sunk Island Review* (England), Spring, 1992
"Slattery Street Crockers" first published in *Qwerty*, 1997
"Two Crosses" first published in *Grain*, Winter, 1989, and *The Australasian Post* (Australia), February, 1995

GRANTS
The author wishes to thank the Canada Council and the Newfoundland and Labrador Arts Council for their continued financial support during the completion of this work.

AWARDS AND SHORT LISTS
"Above the Movements of Night" was awarded the Canadian Author Association's Okanagan Fiction Prize
"Merciful Hope" was short listed for the CBC Literary Award
"The Plastic Superman" was a winner in the fictional prose division of the 1994 Newfoundland Arts & Letters Awards

ANTHOLOGIES
"Behind Glass" was selected for *Hard Times: A New Fiction Anthology*
"The Broken Earth" was chosen to appear in Oberon's *Best Canadian Stories*